DEAD END

ROBBIE DORMAN

Dead End by Robbie Dorman

www.robbiedorman.com

ISBN-13: 978-1-958768-03-7

Cover design by Bukovero

For the regulars.

1

Joe Amery's feet hurt. He'd only been in the warehouse for an hour, and his feet already hurt.

"This is everything here," said Mr. Johnson, who walked with him. They hustled past long lines of conveyor belts, with plastic bins on one, and a lengthy line of boxes on another, and another set of boxes on another.

"That's incoming shipments. They'll get unpacked, scanned, and then the robots will sort them in the right bin," said Johnson. Joe tried to keep his eye on the varying boxes as they walked, but they were moving too fast. "Stow process."

Joe and Mr. Johnson were already past it. They were covering ground quickly, and Joe had worn comfy sneakers like suggested. Didn't matter, though. He hadn't worked on concrete in years, and he knew it would take weeks for his feet to adjust. As much as they could adjust, at least. Human bodies weren't meant for concrete floors.

"Next up is the picking area," said Mr. Johnson, moving fast. He had wasted no time with niceties. Joe had watched introduction videos right after he'd been hired. They hadn't spent any time on that today. You were always on the clock at Nile. "That's where you'll be working."

They passed station after station, all of them with enormous signs with names on them. None of the workers even so much as glanced as the two of them walked by. They were too busy.

Johnson walked them to Station Zeta, which was empty. Joe saw the spring mat that covered the entire area, and his weary feet rejoiced.

"The robots will bring you rows of items in bins, each of them labeled. The computer will tell you what to pick. You find the item, and put it in a tote." He gestured to a yellow plastic box sitting on a conveyor belt in front of him. "You tell the computer you're good, and then you do it again, and again, and again. Understand?"

"I think so," said Joe. It seemed simple.

"Let's try," said Johnson. "I click ready on the computer, and you're off to the races." He clicked, and the robots went to work, a series of shelves on motorized wheels moving around in front of Joe. One finally settled directly ahead of him. He looked at the computer. Headphones, in bin CCC47. His eyes scanned the labels quickly, found the bin, and dug through the handful of items, finding the headphones. They matched the description. He put it in the yellow box, the tote that Mr. Johnson had described.

"Good job," said Johnson, watching. Johnson leaned over and tapped a big green button labeled NEXT, and everything moved. The belt took the tote away, and another set of shelves whirred over to Joe's location. Johnson watched as Joe did it again. This time it was a children's doll, and Joe did the same thing, finding it quickly and moving it to the tote, and then hit the NEXT button himself.

"That's it," said Johnson. "You're a natural."

"Is there anything else?"

"No, that's about it," said Johnson. "The computer has your breaks programmed into it. Any other questions?"

"What do I do if the item isn't in the bin?"

Johnson smiled for the first time. "Report the error, and they'll fix it. But I doubt it will happen. The computer's very smart. Anything else?"

"Where's the bathroom?"

Johnson's smile disappeared. He pointed way down, back to where Joe had entered the massive building. "Back near the break area," said Mr. Johnson. "I tell people to wait for a break, because it'll take you that long to get down there. I'll leave you to it." Mr. Johnson left without a second glance.

Joe got to work. He picked orders as they came, letting his mind wander. His aching feet hurt a little less on the cushioned mat, but they still hurt. He'd have to get insoles to help.

After my first paycheck, I'll buy insoles.

No money in the budget for them now. No money in the budget for much, not until he got his first check in two weeks. He could make it until then. He'd made it this far.

The Nile fulfillment center had seemed so big when he had arrived this morning. Too big, even. It towered over the surrounding landscape. There was debate if it should be built, and eventually Nile won out. Springfield had watched as Nile built, and speculated how long it'd be 'til it opened. It wasn't long.

Joe had debated applying the whole time.

All he read about was how a job working at one of these places was hell, and Nile didn't give one shit about any of its employees. But they were hiring, and they would need thousands of people. He had held out, but then he saw the new bills for his mom, and he had given in, applying on his phone in the middle of the night, lying on Helen's couch as she slept in her bedroom, in what once had been *their* bedroom.

That's why you took the job. Sure, it might be mindless, but it will pay the bills. And with enough time, you can move out on your own again. Get a good night's sleep.

Helen's couch wasn't great, but it was better than the street.

He worked, moving quickly. The job was simple, and he had encountered no errors. His hands swiftly grabbed the needed item from the labeled bin, and moved it to the tote, and the tote disappeared down a conveyor belt, to be put in a box by someone else, and then delivered somewhere later today or tomorrow.

After an hour, his mind wandered.

God, this is boring.

But even with the monotony, the time passed quickly. The pace of the work was fast, and never ending, and his first break came, and he hustled down to the bathroom and rushed back, making it just in time. Then more picking, and then before he knew it, it was time for lunch.

He only had a half hour, and he hurried down to the break room for this section of the compound. He hadn't seen it, but Mr. Johnson had explained that they were sectioned off into smaller areas, the thousands of employees quartered off into smaller groups, never seeing each other, despite all reporting to the same building every day.

Joe grabbed his lunch from the fridge, a bologna sandwich and a bag of chips, plus a cup of water from the cooler. The cafeteria was a madhouse, and Joe took his lunch and got away from it as quickly as he could. He knew no one and went to sit down at an empty table. Joe sat and ate. He spotted a young, blonde woman, wearing a lab coat, eating two tables over. A lab coat?

"New guy?" asked a soft Midwestern voice, and then a man sat down across from him, placing a paper sack on the table. "Alright if I sit here?"

"Uh, sure," said Joe. The man was big, over six feet tall, and probably weighed over 250 pounds. His shoulders were broad, but slightly slumped and his hair was gray and messy, tousled disarray on his head. His smile and eyes were genuine, though, and he fell into the chair. He wore compression sleeves on both elbows. He looked to be in his mid-50s, but it was hard to tell.

"My name's Wally," he said. He extended a hand out to Joe, and Joe took it, shaking. "I know it's old-fashioned to introduce yourself to everyone, and with how many people we go through, Mr. Johnson calls it a waste of time—but I still like to do it. It's good to feel welcome."

"Joe," he said. "Thanks. Uh—how long have you worked here?"

"Oh, three years, right since they opened up," said Wally. "I did phone sales before this, and believe me, everyone says this job is hard, and they're not wrong, but I'd rather put stuff in boxes all day than have to talk people into buying something they don't really need. Here, Nile does all the selling for me."

"So, you like the job?" asked Joe. "All I saw online was about how grueling it is."

"I guess I do," said Wally, answering as if he had never pondered the question before.

"You don't sound so sure."

"Oh, well, who likes their job?" asked Wally, half smiling. He unpacked his lunch, which consisted of an egg salad sandwich, a small package of peanut butter crackers, and a pudding cup. He took a huge bite of his sandwich, chewed once, twice, and then swallowed. "They call it work for a reason, right?"

"I guess so."

"I've never thought about it being something to love, or even like," said Wally. "I need the money, so I work. But I've had worse jobs."

Joe eyed the blonde woman again, past Wally. Wally glanced back.

"One of the scientists," said Wally. "Best to just leave them alone."

"What do you mean, leave them alone?"

"In my experience, none of them will talk to us," said Wally. "Don't blame them. They live in a different world from us."

"Surprised she's here, eating with the rabble."

"People get lonely," said Wally, chewing.

"Any advice?" asked Joe. Wally took another bite, and his

sandwich was gone, and as he chewed, he was opening the crackers.

"Eat faster," said Wally, smiling, shoving crackers into his mouth.

"Half hour isn't long, especially with how long it takes to get to the lunch area," said Joe.

"You're not kidding," said Wally. "But I don't need more time at work, anyway. I'd say take care of your feet, of your joints. I use these compression sleeves, and they help when I swell up. Keep your head down, and work as fast as you can. Mr. Johnson, he ain't a bad guy, but he'll put pressure on you to work faster. Don't blame him, I know he's got some guy on top of him, telling him the same thing. You're young, I'm sure you can keep up."

"I hope so," said Joe. The crackers were gone then, too, and the pudding cup was open. Joe was still working on his sandwich, and had just opened his chips.

"It can get pretty boring," said Wally. "My only complaint, really. I just tell myself stories, to pass the time."

"Stories?"

"Oh yeah," said Wally. "Just make 'em up, as I go. Makes things go quicker. But there's way worse things in the world than being bored."

The pudding cup was gone then, with a plastic spoon that Wally tossed into the paper bag along with the empty cup.

"But mainly, I'd suggest you eat faster," said Wally, smiling, and then winked. "I gotta get back to work. Here, kid." He handed Joe a napkin. "That's my number, if you want to get a beer."

"Ah, thanks."

"No worries," said Wally, pushing himself out of his chair, his big body moving slowly. Joe heard his knees pop, and then Wally was up, and he suddenly moved quickly, dropping his lunch bag in the trash and walking with purpose out of the cafeteria.

Joe glanced at the clock and realized he only had ten minutes left for his lunch. It'd take five minutes of fast walking just to get back to his station so he could punch back in. He hurried his eating, forcing down his sandwich and chips. Wally's advice was better than it seemed.

He finished in time and clocked in just under a half hour. He started working again, moving item from place to place. Time didn't move as quickly in the second half of his shift. His feet, ankles, and knees ached, even on the cushy mat he stood on. The lack of music, and the clatter of the warehouse, of the constant noise on the PA, of machines turning and spinning and stamping, filled his ears.

How many days of this would there be? Wally had done three years so far. Would he be able to stomach this job for that long?

Think about Mom. She needs you, more than ever.

And so Joe did. He thought about his mother. He'd go and see her tonight. It'd been a few weeks. He knew she was lonely at the home, even after she'd made friends there. Now that he had the job, he could give her some good news.

And then his shift was over.

First day done.

Joe stood outside, as everyone on his shift filtered out, and all the people in the next filtered in, going through the metal detectors. He looked up at the enormous building. It was so, so big.

"Best not to think about it too much, kid," said Wally, walking up next to him.

"Think about what?"

"About how small we are," said Wally. "Compared to it. Only makes you feel bad."

"More advice?"

"Yeah, I guess," said Wally. "I'd still say you should just focus on eating faster. Easier to control."

2

"Would you help me put on my socks, honey? It's a little harder than it used to be."

Joe's mom sat in her easy chair, a big recliner that Joe had found on a free furniture Facebook group. He had mended the fabric where it had been torn in the back and it worked, good as new. He slid the thick, warm socks over his mom's feet, pulling them up as far as he could.

His mother had always been a large woman, but never overweight. She was tall, nearly six feet, with broad shoulders and big hips, but had been on her feet her entire life, working in restaurants. Even as she aged, the work had kept the weight off. But when the medical problems hit, she had to stop working, and without the constant exercise, the weight packed on. Her walker sat next to the recliner, folded in half, ready for use.

He hated to look at it.

"Oh, thank you. My feet were getting pretty cold."

Joe stood up and walked over to the smaller chair in the corner, taking a seat. His mom's room wasn't huge, but it seemed big enough, with a bed, a moderately sized television, turned to the home and garden channel. There was a kitchenette, with a small fridge, a microwave, and a toaster oven.

A door led to her bathroom.

It seemed big enough, until you had to live there for the rest of your life.

"I'm so glad you visited," said Mom, a smile lifting the corners of her sad eyes. "I was just thinking about you the other day, and I was going to call you, but I figured you were busy."

"You can always call me," said Joe. "If I'm busy, I won't answer. I'll call you back."

"Oh, I know," she said. "I just don't want to be a burden."

"Mom," said Joe. "You're not a burden."

And she wasn't. Sure, the reason he was desperate for work, and frantically digging himself out of a mountain of debt was because of how much this place cost, on top of having to feed and take care of himself. The retirement home was expensive, even if it wasn't top of the line, but his mom had spent her whole life doing the same for him.

It was his time to take care of her. Even if it killed him.

"You know, I don't have to be here," she said. "I could fend for myself living with you. I don't need a nurse, or a doctor on call, it seems—"

"Mom," said Joe. "You know I can't take care of you." And

he couldn't. After all her medical issues, he wasn't enough. And maybe some nights she didn't need the nurse or doctor on call. But some nights, she'd wake up and need a shot or an IV drip and he couldn't handle that. He wasn't a nurse.

"But this place is so expensive," she said. "And I miss—"

She trailed off, but Joe knew what she would say. She missed being independent.

"Believe me," he said. "If I could get you out of here, with at-home care, I would." But he didn't even have a place of his own. His mom stared out the window. He took a breath. "I got a new job."

She looked at him. "Oh, that's great news, honey. What is it?"

"It's working in the Nile Fulfillment Center," said Joe. "My first day was today. It's the huge building, off the highway outside of town."

"Nile?" asked Mom. "I just saw something in the news about them—something about their owner, and some scandal—"

"Yeah, I think it was insider trading this time," said Joe. He honestly didn't know. It was one of the thousand reasons he hadn't wanted to work for Nile. But who else was he going to work for? Walmart? Costco? All the same problems. At least this job paid better, and he didn't have to talk to customers.

"That's not good," said Mom.

"Above my pay grade," said Joe, with a half smile. "It pays pretty well."

"Really?"

"Yeah," said Joe. "I'm hoping—I'm hoping this one will stick. Work there a couple years, and get back on my feet.

And get you out of here."

Her eyes lit up. "Joe, you don't have to—"

"I know you don't like it here. And I don't blame you. But I'll get you out. I promise." His mom looked away, tears in her eyes. She wiped at them with a spare tissue. Joe got up and went to her, hugging her. She hugged him back.

"It's not that bad," she said. "It's just not how I thought I'd spend my golden years, you know? I always pictured a community in Florida, or on a beach somewhere. That's what they told us, when we were younger. That if we worked hard, and saved up, we'd retire to a beach somewhere."

Joe only squeezed her harder.

*

Helen sat on their couch when he got home. Well, *her* couch.

Keep it straight, Joe. It was always hers.

She glanced up at him when he came in, and then her eyes went back to the TV.

"How was your first day?" she asked.

"It was alright," said Joe. "It's hard work. Boring. But nothing crazy."

"There's some extra mac and cheese in the fridge, if you want it."

"I mean, yeah, if you're offering," said Joe. His stomach had been growling for hours. Bologna sandwiches had been keeping him alive for months now. He walked to the fridge and grabbed the tupperware with macaroni in it and a fork, and sat down at the bar, eating right away.

"Not gonna heat it up?"

"I like it cold," said Joe, devouring the food. He hadn't realized how hungry he was. Standing on his feet all day had burned a lot of calories.

"You going to keep this one?"

"I'm going to try," said Joe. "The pay is good. Hours are hard, but I can do it."

"Was that ever the problem?" asked Helen. Her question hung in the air, and Joe felt some of the condescension in her voice. No, he wouldn't get into an argument with her, not again.

"A couple months of paychecks, and I should be able to get out of your hair," said Joe, answering a different question.

"A couple months?" asked Helen. "So what, June? July?"

"Maybe," said Joe. "I want to get an apartment, and set my mom up there with me."

"You'll be able to save up that much in two months?"

"You want me out of here or not?" asked Joe. He felt his temper rising. She always questioned him. She never trusted him.

"I do," said Helen. "But I also don't want you to tell me you'll be out in two months and then in two months you tell me it'll be another two months. I want you to commit to something."

"Then sure, two months."

"Have you crunched the numbers, or are you just hoping and wishing that two months will be enough time—"

"I worked all day, Helen," said Joe. "Do you expect me to do the math while I'm working?"

Helen sighed. "No, but instead of guessing a number, you could tell me the truth, and say I don't know, I *will* do that math, and get back to you."

Joe took a deep breath. "I don't even have a paycheck yet," he said. "Can I get paid first, please?"

"Fine," said Helen, looking back at the TV. "Let's hope you get one this time."

"What the hell is that supposed to mean?"

"This is the third time we've had this conversation, Joe."

"Those weren't my fault."

"Yeah, I know," said Helen. "I remember how the foreman of the construction job with benefits was mean to you, so you quit—"

"He was a homophobe, Helen, what the hell was I supposed—"

"And then I got you the job with my company, and you blew up at your boss for asking you to stay late—"

"He was an asshole—"

"I don't care, Joe," said Helen. "Is this better now? Working for Nile?"

Joe took a deep breath. "No one should have to take poor treatment from a job just to keep their roof over their head. It's not right, I'm a human, not some machine—"

"What world do you live in?" asked Helen. "You think you're special?"

"You're one to talk, you haven't had to face it like I have—"

"Excuse me?" asked Helen. "Face what, Joe? Someone being mean to you? Being a cog in the machine? You're smart, smarter than me—"

"Stop this—"

"But you can't stay in one place. You're looking for some utopia that will never exist—"

"You work for those monsters," said Joe. "You're lecturing me, while you work for—"

"They're *all* monsters," said Helen, her voice cold. "You show me a job, if you trace it back high enough, there's some Patrick Bateman motherfucker sitting at the top of it, collecting money, and paying you a small pittance."

"I don't want to just accept that as a fact of life!" yelled Joe. He didn't want to yell, he didn't, but it came out of him, fire from his lungs.

"I don't like it, Joe," said Helen. "But I do pay my bills. Please, figure out your plan, and tell me what it is. I'm not going to kick you out into the street, but I'd prefer to have my couch back."

"It used to be our couch," said Joe.

"Maybe," said Helen. "Maybe once. But not anymore."

Joe took a deep breath, and he wanted to scream, he wanted to be alone, but there was nowhere in Helen's apartment to be alone, and so he left, shutting the front door behind him, and he walked down to his car, the hood still warm, and got inside.

He had nowhere to go. No sanctuary.

Helen didn't understand, couldn't understand.

Joe pulled out his phone and found Wally's number.

Joe texted him. *Hey, want to get a drink?*

3

Joe didn't spot Wally at first. He saw the dog first, a fluffy corgi, patiently laying down underneath the table at the booth in the corner. And then he saw Wally's crooked grin as Wally waved him over.

The dive bar was called The Tin Nickel, a little hole in the wall place that was a fifteen minute drive from Helen's apartment. It was right around the corner from Wally's house. A beer sat in front of Wally, half drank. Another sat across from him.

"I ordered one for you," said Wally. "Hope you don't mind Fat Tire."

"You didn't have to—"

Wally waved him off. "I know you don't get paid for two weeks, so don't worry about it. You can owe me one, down the road."

"Well, thank you," said Joe, sitting down. "They allow dogs in here?"

"No," said Wally, grinning. "No dogs allowed. But Betsy, she's the exception that proves the rule. This is her booth."

"Is that right?" asked Joe. He looked down at the dog, who looked at him with a smile, her tongue hanging out the side of her mouth. He scratched her behind the ear, and her tail wagged lazily. "Well, thank you for letting me sit at your booth, Betsy."

Joe sat back against the wooden seat and took a long swig of beer. It was cold and felt nice. The bar was quiet on a weeknight, an unrecognizable country song warbling on low volume from the jukebox.

"You alright?" asked Wally. "You look like you're carrying a heavy load. First day went okay, right?"

"As well as it could," said Joe. "I had a fight with my ex, and—and I'm just tired."

"You want to talk about it?"

"There's nothing to talk about," said Joe. "She wants me out the door, and anything I say that isn't 'I'm leaving' is only going to make things worse."

"Why don't you leave?"

"No place to go," said Joe. "Things went bad while we were dating. Been sleeping on the couch while I'm trying to get back on my feet."

"Well, you've got work now," said Wally. "Just keep at it, and things will look up again. Just keep working. Before you know it, you'll have your own place again. You seem like you have a good head on your shoulders. Things will work out."

"You get all that after a conversation at lunch?"

"Well, yeah," said Wally. "How many of our co-workers have you talked to?"

"I said hello to a couple of people today, but other than that, it's only you."

"Well, Nile doesn't have very strict requirements for working in the warehouse, and yes, after a couple conversations you're already in the top percentile of most agreeable. Most people who come through are only there for a week or two, and then they're gone, for whatever reason. And that's the people who will actually talk to you. Some of them— man, they must have something wrong, because they give you the stink eye just for saying hello."

"You're friendly, Wally," said Joe. "Some people don't trust that. Think you're trying to sell them something. Or get one over on them."

Wally shook his head. "All we have is each other."

Joe took a swallow of beer. "You ever have doubts working for Nile?"

"What do you mean?"

"I mean, they do lots of bad stuff," said Joe. "The fact they exist at all puts a lot of small mom and pop shops out of business."

"I don't think about it."

"At all?" asked Joe.

"Nope," said Wally. "What's the point?"

"I just try and be thoughtful about my decisions," said Joe. "About what I interact with, and how it reflects on me."

"I'm an old man," said Wally. "So I'm speaking from experience—none of that makes a difference."

"I don't want to be a person who doesn't care about that

stuff."

"Well, there you go. That's a different thing altogether. That's about deciding who you think you are, but nothing about actually changing the world. Because we're too small, man. Just too small. And I gotta eat, and I need clothes, and I need food for Betsy. And I could spend the extra money every time to make sure my clothes are ethically sourced, or that my dog food isn't from GMO cows, whatever the hell that means, but in the end, it's costing me a bunch of money and doesn't make one lick of difference to the big boys. They are the ocean, and me not shopping at them, or working for them—it doesn't affect them."

"But, if we got enough people, doing the same thing—"

"Different thing. That's organized action. That's a boycott. Are you organizing a boycott?"

"Well, no," said Joe.

"Of course you're not," said Wally. "I'm not either. Because who the hell has time for that? I'm working sixty-hour weeks, and that's just to keep Betsy and me fed. But without a massive organized effort, none of it makes a big enough difference. Especially without the government getting involved."

Joe sighed and took a swig of beer. "That feels very defeating."

"That's why I don't think about it," said Wally. "I've made my bed, man. I'm working for Nile, and I make due. The job sucks, but most warehouse jobs suck. This is one of the better ones, honestly."

"You *have* thought about it."

"There's a lot of time at the picking station to think," said Wally. "Lot of time to think at most of the jobs I've had."

"You seem like a smart guy," said Joe. "How'd you end up here?"

"I'd ask you the same question."

"Bad luck."

"I've had my fair share," said Wally. "Just when I'm about to get my head above water, the car breaks down. Or I need a new roof. Or poor Betsy swallows a tennis ball. And then I'm sinking again. Fighting the tides."

"I was in college," said Joe. "Was going to get an English degree. Then my mom got sick. Had to drop out to help her."

"I left to follow my girlfriend," said Wally. "Thought it was true love, figured I could pick up the rest of college somewhere else. Well—it wasn't true love, and I didn't pick up anything except a bunch of different jobs over the years." He finished off his beer, and within moments, the waitress had brought over another for both of them. She pet Betsy and then walked off again.

"That's some good service."

"Betsy sweet-talked it for us," said Wally, winking, before taking a sip from his new beer.

The beer was taking effect on Joe. The tension in his shoulders eased, just a little.

"I don't blame Helen," said Joe. "She let me stay with her even after we broke up. But she doesn't understand. Her dad was a lawyer, and even if something went wrong—"

"She always had a cushion to land on, right?"

"Yeah," said Joe. "Flying on the fucking trapeze without a safety net. That's my life."

"If I had my say, of course there wouldn't be mega corporations, run by assholes who're ruining the world. I'd snap my fingers, and everything would be hunky dory," said Wally. "But I don't have a say. And neither do you. This job ain't going anywhere, and as long as you show up and work hard, they'll keep you around. It's hard work, but you'll make good money, especially with the mandatory overtime."

"See, that's what I mean, mandatory overtime, what the hell is that, it's bullshit—"

Wally held up a finger. "Saying things like that will get you fired. And yes, I agree, it is bullshit. But do you want to get out of your ex's apartment? Then you stay silent, and you do what you're told."

Joe sighed again and finished his first beer. "I've never been able to do that."

"I know," said Wally. "I was the same way for a long time. But this is the world we live in. Make peace with it, because it ain't changing, at least not for the better."

They chatted for a while, each of their beers getting lower. Wally let Joe take Betsy for a walk around the block so she could do her business, and Betsy trotted along, smelling along the street, looking for a place to squat.

Joe stared at the dog. She was oblivious to all of this. To her, life was peeing, and pooping, and eating, and sleeping, and getting pets. The night air was cool, and all the earlier anger and frustration at Helen was gone. The beer had helped. Plus the talk with Wally. Petting Betsy hadn't hurt either.

But some of it was also having a plan. Wally was right, that this job wasn't going anywhere. It wouldn't get yanked out from under him. If he could keep his mouth shut and toe the line, he could stick to this job. He would make some money and get him and his mom in a good place. Maybe—maybe he could patch things up with Helen. He still loved her, despite everything. Maybe without all the stress about money, they could fix things.

Betsy did her business on a fire hydrant, and he walked her back to the bar, where Wally sat in the same place. Betsy fluffed her way to him and sat down at his feet, in the same spot she was at before.

"Everything alright?" asked Wally.

"Yeah, she did her thing."

"How about with you?"

"Yeah, I think so," said Joe. "Just have to keep my head on straight. God, waiting for my first check will be miserable."

"Always the hardest one," said Wally. He looked at Joe with a question in his eyes.

"What is it?" asked Joe. "There's something you're not telling me."

"They told me to keep it on the down low," said Wally. "The HR person at Nile. Said it was an exclusive opportunity, whatever the hell that means. But someone told me, so I'll tell you. The R&D lab has some job openings, and they only want people who work at the fulfillment center to apply. Said they had to have experience working at Nile."

"But they didn't come to you?" asked Joe.

"I think they're expecting word to travel," said Wally. "And it's working, I guess. But it's a promotion. Pay is double what you make in the fulfillment center."

"Double? Holy shit," said Joe. "What, like $40 an hour?"

"Yeah," said Wally. "And that's before overtime. But I put in for it, and got interviewed. And it went pretty well, I think. But show up a few minutes early tomorrow, and talk to HR, if you're interested."

"What kind of work is it?"

"I don't know," said Wally. "They said they need to test some new efficiency measures. Nile has always been on the cutting edge at their fulfillment centers. That's why they've been so successful. And I guess they're pushing even harder in that direction. But they couldn't tell me more. That I would find out if I got the promotion."

"I mean, it can't hurt to put in for it, right?"

"That's what I said," said Wally. "And if I get it, hell, I can finally get Betsy that doghouse she's been wanting, with the built-in heater." Betsy looked up at the mention of her name and licked Wally's hand.

"I think that's enough for me," said Joe, finishing his second beer. "Helen has probably cooled down by now. Thank you for the beers. I owe you."

"You owe Betsy," said Wally. "It's her booth, don't forget."

4

"You're late, Amery," said Mr. Johnson, as Joe clocked in on the computer, getting his station up and moving. "And we're running behind today. Already we're in neck deep—"

"Sorry, Mr. Johnson," said Joe. "I was applying for the promotion to R&D, and I tried to get here early, but the metal detector line was really long, a couple people were trying to get through with their phones, and it held everyone up—"

"Wait, you're applying for the promotion?" asked Johnson. His face changed, the anger disappearing. "Well, never mind then. Good luck."

"So I'm okay?"

"Yeah, there's a big push to get guys into the lab," said Johnson. "So don't worry about it. But we are behind, so do your best today."

"10-4," said Joe, and started working, the great machine turning over, with shelves full of products flowing to him, and him grabbing the proper thing, and moving it to another bin, and the bin sailing away on a conveyor belt, only to repeat it, over and over again. His feet and shins ached after only an hour, still tender from the previous days. He dry swallowed the ibuprofen he had pocketed at Helen's. They would help dull the ache and get him through the day.

The HR rep had been happy to put Joe's name on the list for R&D. The "exclusive opportunity" must have just been the interviewer selling it to Wally, because it didn't seem that surprising for Joe to be putting his name in. There had even been a line at the door, and most of what Joe could hear from the few ahead of him were the same. The amount of money they were paying had spread far and wide quickly, and money talked.

HR had told him they'd interview him within a week or two, and he'd know if he got the promotion a week after that. He had more questions, but he was already late at that point and he had to run.

But his normal work continued, and he became a machine, processing order after order. After a few hours music turned on, the first time it happened, a contemporary hits station, and even that made the work so much better. Why couldn't they play the music all the time?

Because they save it for when they need a carrot.

Johnson had said they were behind on orders for the day, and playing the music would make people work harder. And if they played it all the time, it would be something the workers would expect.

Joe cursed under his breath, and then tried his best to push it out of his mind, like Wally had said. Don't think about it. Do your work. Sure, when there's no music it's boring as fuck, but there's music now. Take advantage of it.

And Joe did, despite himself, and he moved faster. He looked at the clock, and was stunned to realize it was lunchtime. He hadn't seen Wally today, and he hoped to see him at lunch, at least to say hi. Their conversation really had helped. It helped to hear someone older who had faced the same problems he had.

Wally wasn't in the cafeteria when Joe arrived, and so Joe sat down, and thought to Wally's other advice, to eat quickly, and Joe ate, eating big bites of his bologna sandwich.

And then he saw her. The same woman from yesterday, the woman from R&D, the scientist, eating with them. He remembered Wally's words, to leave her be, but then she made eye contact with him again, and smiled.

If she worked in R&D, maybe she would have info about the jobs available there. Couldn't hurt to ask, could it?

He got up and walked to her.

"Anyone sitting here?" he asked, gesturing to the seat across from her.

"Uh, no—"

"Great," he said. He sat down. "Hi, I'm Joe."

"Oh, hi," she said. "I'm Anna."

"Is it true?" he asked.

"Is what true?"

"That you work for R&D."

"Yeah, I do," she said. Her eyes caught his, and then went back to her food, a small salad in front of her.

"I hear they're hiring."

"They are?"

"Yeah, my buddy Wally had an interview the other day," said Joe. "I applied this morning. Don't have an interview yet, though."

"Oh, right, of course," said Anna. "Sorry, I wasn't thinking straight."

"They're not giving us much info about the positions. Do you know anything about that?"

"I really can't say," said Anna. "I'm not in charge of hiring anyone. I just work there." Her eyes told a different story. She wouldn't look at him for more than a second or two. Why was she so nervous?

"Oh, of course," said Joe. "What kind of work do you do?"

"Oh, it's all about efficiency."

"That's what my buddy told me," said Joe. "But what does that mean?"

Anna eyed him again, for a moment, and then looked away. "I don't know if I should say anything. Nile is very serious about leaks—"

"Oh, I won't tell anyone. Who would I tell?"

"I shouldn't," said Anna.

"So you don't talk to anyone about work?"

"Not really," said Anna. "I don't talk to many people."

"You don't have friends?" asked Joe. "Family?"

"I moved here from out of state for my job," said Anna. "So my family is back in Florida. And I don't really have any friends here."

"None?" asked Joe. "I mean, I'll be your friend."

"We just met—"

"I just met Wally the other day and he's my friend," said

Joe. "All we have is each other."

Anna's eyes widened then, and stared at him for a moment, the first time she'd made eye contact and kept it. And then she broke it, and grabbed her salad, standing up, the chair scraping against the floor.

"I'm sorry, I can't," she said. "I've got to go. I'm late for a meeting." And then she walked away without looking back, hurrying around and through the people waiting at the vending machines. She exited through a different door, waving a key card at a scanner and then hastily moving through it.

What the hell was that about?

Must have been something he said. He looked at his watch and realized he only had five minutes to get back to work. Joe shoveled the rest of his food into his mouth and hurried back to his workstation. He made it just under the wire.

Music wasn't playing anymore.

They must have caught up on orders.

Or at least that's what Joe suspected. He didn't see Mr. Johnson for the rest of the day. I'm sure he might, if he slowed down, but Joe didn't slow down. He continued at the same pace, taking more ibuprofen as his feet swelled in his shoes.

This was the worst time, in the mid-afternoon, when he still had hours to go, and nothing but the work to keep him busy, and the hours stretched on, and he was tired, an hour of missed sleep here or there catching up to him. It was when it was harder to shoulder the burden of the knowledge that the job was using him. That it viewed him as disposable.

All of his jobs had been this way, as far back as he could

remember. Even the steady jobs, or the ones he liked more than most, he still knew that he was a cog in the machine, a pawn, a tool for his bosses. They cared as much as they needed to, but there was never a moment that Joe could forget that if he got sick, they would replace him in a moment.

It was hard to forget. It's what happened to his mom. She had worked at the restaurant for years, The Grand, a fancy restaurant in a classy hotel. She waited tables, and then moved up to host, and then finally behind the scenes, as a manager. It had taken her decades of working on her feet to get there, of carrying trays, all the while raising Joe alone, his dad dead when he was little. Years and years of loyal service to the restaurant, working whenever they needed someone, when someone else called in, when her toes bled because she was on her feet too long that day.

And then she got sick.

Breast cancer. She couldn't work while doing radiation and chemo, but there was no sick leave. They didn't hold her spot while she got better. No. They fired her, replaced her, and they left her with nothing, no insurance, no support. All because of greed. Because she was an expendable line item.

So, she suffered alone. Well, with Joe. But there was no one else, and a lifetime of saving and scrimping vanished in a year. His mom survived, but with a slate of minor health issues that kept her from working ever again, leaving Joe with the need to care for her and for himself.

It bled into everything. Why he couldn't hold a job for long, for a week, or a few months, or maybe even a couple years, before that knowledge crept up on him. Everyone knew they were disposable, knew they weren't important, but they didn't act like him. They smiled at the boss, and did what they were told, even when they hated it.

Joe couldn't. He couldn't look that hypocrisy in the face and smile. It would wear on him wherever he went. He only saw his mother's sad face as she was fired over the phone, as chemicals dripped into her arm, to both kill her and keep her breathing.

He pushed it all away, trying to empty his mind as he worked. Joe focused only on the task at hand. He thought about Anna, the strange scientist, friendly at first, but then distant. Wally, his new friend, and his adorable dog. How he would fix things with Helen. His mother. About where they could live together, where he could afford a roof, and food, and at-home care for her, on just the salary of a fulfillment center worker.

Maybe he could make it work, if he worked all the overtime he could, and cut every corner he found.

But maybe he couldn't. Maybe it was a fool's errand to think it was possible at all.

The thought of $40 an hour working in the R&D lab became more and more attractive. Sure, they were being dodgy about what the work was, but with that kind of money, he could afford his own place. That was more than Helen made. It would sort out a lot of problems.

And then he realized his shift was over, and relief filled him. He clocked out, and left as quickly as he could, going through the rigmarole of the metal detector and the pat downs.

"Joe!" a voice yelled as he walked to his car. Joe turned. It was Wally.

"Hey," said Joe. "Glad I could catch you today. What you

said last night—"

"I got the promotion!" said Wally, patting Joe on the arm. Wally smiled. "I got the position in R&D."

"That's great," said Joe. "I'm happy for you."

"I'm jacked, man," said Wally. "I start tomorrow. They want me in as quick as possible. Have you put in?"

"Yeah, this morning," said Joe.

"Oh, great," said Wally. "Once I'm in, I'll put in the good word. All we have is each other."

"Amen," said Joe. "Amen."

5

The interview was the next day.

Joe was working as normal when he was taken aside by his boss, who led him to a small meeting room with a table and two chairs, one on each side.

A bald man in a suit sat on the other side and smiled widely as Joe entered. Mr. Johnson closed the door as he left.

"Joe Amery?" asked the man.

"That's me," said Joe.

"Excellent," said the man. "Please, have a seat."

Joe sat down across from him. "And your name?"

"Oh, I'm Mr. William Boggins," he said, smiling again. Joe looked at him and had a hard time with his face. It seemed to resent Joe looking. He glanced away. "I'm the company representative for Research and Development.

You showed interest in opportunities opening up for Fulfill-ment Center employees?"

"Yes," said Joe. "Though details were a little sparse about what the job would entail."

"Where did you hear about the position?"

"Oh, through the grapevine," said Joe. He remembered Wally saying the job was hush hush. He didn't want to get him in trouble.

Boggins took notes, writing quickly in a notebook.

"So, what does the job entail?"

"Please, I'd ask you to hold your questions until the end of the interview," said Boggins, still staring at his notes. "There will be plenty of time to answer them then."

Joe resisted saying something smart, instead just sitting in silence, as Boggins wrote. The noise of his pen scratch-ing against the paper filled the room. Finally, he looked up again.

"How old are you?"

"I'm 32," said Joe. "Don't you already have this informa-tion?"

"Just verifying everything for our records," said Boggins. "I appreciate your patience. 32. Your only relative is your mother?"

"Well, yes," said Joe. "What does that have to do with anything?"

"Please, Mr. Amery," said Boggins. "We need as much data as possible. It absolutely pertains to the position, be-lieve me. Do you live with her?"

"No," said Joe. "I live with a roommate."

"Hrmm," murmured Boggins, making more notes. His eyes danced back over Joe, and it was unwelcome. Joe suddenly felt like he was being examined. "How has the fulfillment center job treated you so far?"

"Alright," said Joe. "It's a little boring, but otherwise fine."

"Not too hard on you?"

"No, not really," said Joe. "Some normal aches and pains from being on my feet all day, but that's typical. Nothing too bad. Ibuprofen takes care of it."

"And no history of other medical problems?"

Joe only stared at him.

"Mr. Amery?"

"Why do you need my medical history?"

Boggins stared back at him, and this time Joe didn't look away.

"Why do you want this position, Mr. Amery?"

"I hear it pays well. Double what the fulfillment center pays. Is that true?"

"Yes," said Boggins. "It is. It pays over double what the fulfillment center pays. It's quite generous." Boggins' stare didn't break. "If you want to be considered for the position, you must answer my questions. If you don't wish to answer them, you may return to work. Mr. Johnson mentioned you're behind on orders, I'm sure he'll appreciate you back there—"

Frustration and anger bubbled up in Joe's mind.

Play nice. You want Mom out of the home? You want your own place?

"No medical history, no," said Joe, finally, pushing the anger deep down inside. Boggins held his gaze for a moment longer and then returned to his notepad.

"And in your family?"

"Mother is a breast cancer survivor. Father died in a car

accident when I was young. Don't know about my grandparents. Never met them."

Boggins nodded.

"No history of smoking?"

"No."

"Alcohol?"

"A beer now and then."

"Do you have a close knit friend group?"

"I don't know what that means," said Joe.

"Do you have a small, close circle of friends, or do you associate with a bigger group of people on a shallower level?"

"The second one."

The questions came, over and over, for over an hour.

"Do you go out often?"

"Have you ever bitten by a snake?"

"Do you have social media profiles?"

The questions came, and Joe answered them all. He didn't know why Nile wanted all this information before they hired him or not, but he had pursued this job, and so he answered them.

He dodged a few, giving incomplete information, and he outright lied about a few more, but only on things they could never catch him on.

Had Wally answered all these questions? Boggins continued, tirelessly asking question after question to Joe, taking notes after each, his pen scribbling away.

Finally, he stopped.

"Any questions for me?" asked Boggins, smiling widely again.

"What *is* the job?" asked Joe. "What will I be doing?"

"You'll be working closely with our team in R&D. They are researching innovative techniques to improve efficiency, help employee workflow, and move Nile to a cleaner and faster workplace."

"What does that mean, Mr. Boggins?"

"The team needs workers to consult," said Boggins. "They haven't done the work themselves, so they need outside perspectives to help inform the directions they take. They're very smart people, but they've never worked in a fulfillment center themselves. You'll be providing a fresh point of view and helping guide their research."

"And that's worth $40 an hour?"

"Well, yes," said Boggins. "Some of this technology will guide the company for years to come, and you and your co-workers will help shape it. Some of our previous research has been implemented and iterated upon in our fulfillment centers throughout the world, and often has become industry standard, used even by some of our competitors."

"So, I'll be a consultant?"

"Of sorts," said Boggins. "I can't go into further detail as it would break NDA and confidentiality agreements. If you don't get the job, we can't have you taking the information to others. You understand."

"I guess so," said Joe. He looked at Boggins again, trying to read him. Boggins' face was inscrutable.

But Joe knew he was hiding *something,* and it was more than just information they didn't want their competitors knowing. He was hiding something else.

"What are the hours like?"

"They vary, but typically 40-50 hours," said Boggins. "Overtime included, at time and a half."

Joe did the math in his head. Ten hours a week at $60 an hour. $600 in overtime alone, *every week*. He'd never made that much money. Even if he'd finished his degree—there was no way.

It seemed too good to be true.

"When will I hear back?" asked Joe.

*

We'll be in touch had been Boggins' reply, and Joe had gone back to his workstation. He would have to ask Wally.

He had hoped to catch up with Wally at lunch that day, but Wally wasn't in the cafeteria when Joe took his break. No sign of Anna, the scientist, either. Joe ate alone, and ate quickly. He made it back to his workstation with time to spare.

Work was boring, but consistent, and Joe made it to the end of day, facing down the boredom of the afternoon successfully. It wasn't so bad when he had things to think about. And he definitely had things to think about today.

Mostly, he thought about all the questions they had asked him. So many questions.

Now that he was out of the room, and away from the unreadable face of Mr. Boggins, Joe could actually reflect on them.

And he realized only *some* of them were important. That the number of questions was a smokescreen, just another way for the company to hide what their intentions were. Did they really need to know if he'd been snakebitten before if he was just going to be a consultant?

No, of course not. It was just a way for them to obscure

the info they really wanted, that they needed.

They had asked a lot of medical questions. And a lot of questions about his friends and family.

But why? Joe couldn't piece it together, no matter how much he thought about it. And part of it was that number, the amount of money he'd be making if he got the job. Even as he pondered all those questions the company asked, those numbers intruded. He remembered Helen's words, about doing the math. And he'd done some rudimentary research on the cost of a two-bedroom apartment. Of in-home nursing care.

And it was expensive, probably too much for his current job. He could afford an apartment of his own, and still pay for his mom in the home, but just barely.

With her and daily nurse visits? Not a chance.

But with this job, he could. He could afford it and more. With insurance, and savings, he could dig his way out of the debt, and then actually build a nest egg. Nile had a 401k program, too.

You don't have anything yet. Stop dreaming.

But the dreams intruded.

Don't forget about Boggins' face. And don't forget you thought it was too good to be true.

Boggins was hiding something from him. And Joe wanted to know what it was before he got hired, not after. And Boggins sure as hell wouldn't tell him.

He'd have to ask Wally.

Joe texted him in the parking lot, sitting in his car.

Hey man, how was your first day in the new job?

Joe waited a while. He realized he had no idea what Wally's hours were in the new position. Wally might still be on the clock, for all he knew.

Joe waited for a response, giving him fifteen minutes.

But nothing came. Joe drove back to Helen's. Still nothing.

Wally didn't respond that night.

Or the day after.

Or any time that week.

6

Joe stared at the clock. Fifteen minutes until five.

Half of the office was already gone, having packed up and headed home for the holiday weekend. Of course, they had also come in early, and clocked out early, so they could get a jump on traffic. But Helen liked going in on the later side, and they rode together. Still, only fifteen more minutes.

He stared at the clock, moving his mouse around. It didn't make any sense to start anything now, not when he was going to leave soon, and with a last glance around, he started packing up his things into his backpack. He shoved his empty lunch box into it, along with his tablet, and zipped it up.

When he sat back up, his boss stood next to his desk.

"Mr. Amery," said Mr. Dorning. "Packing up already?"

Joe looked at Mr. Dorning, the fluorescent lights beaming off his bald head, his small mustache tight to his lip. Joe withheld a sigh.

"Well, yes, Mr. Dorning," said Joe. "It's almost five, and I—"

"Are there still active reports in the queue?"

"Well, yes," said Joe. "But there are always active reports in the queue. There's nothing urgent—"

"Did you not see the email I sent out today?"

"Yes," said Joe. "But I thought you were only talking about urgent reports, and I took care of all the urgent reports—"

"Did I specify urgent reports?"

"I—I don't know, I'd have to look again," said Joe. "If you give me a second—"

"I did not specify urgent reports," said Mr. Dorning. "The email said I wanted the active report queue cleared before the holiday weekend."

"But I'm the only person on the team left, it would take me hours to clear out the queue—"

"I think you just answered your own question, then," said Dorning.

"With all due respect, it's a holiday weekend, and I—"

"I thought you understood the responsibilities of taking a salaried position," said Dorning. "And part of that responsibility is working past five o'clock. Working until the job is done."

Joe felt heat rush into his face. His eyes caught the clock turn over to five. The active report queue was in the double digits. He'd be here another three hours, maybe four, if he was going to clear it out. And it didn't matter, none of the reports were urgent, they could all wait until Tuesday—

"Mr. Amery?" asked Dorning. "Am I understood?"

Joe exhaled then, unable to hold it in.

"No, I don't think you are," said Joe. "Why do they need to be done now? They can all wait until next week—"

"I want the queue cleared before the holiday weekend, it's as simple as that."

"It's a three-day weekend," said Joe. "I've been working ten-hour days for weeks now—"

"Mr. Amery, we all work long days—"

"And maybe we all shouldn't," said Joe. "All of this can wait until next week—"

"Mr. Amery, this isn't a request," said Dorning. "If you value this company—"

"Value this company?" asked Joe. The heat rose into his chest. He wanted to go home, he had done exactly what was asked of him. "I get paid thirty-five grand a year. Is the CEO still here? Did he even come in today? You don't have to answer, because I already know it, and no, he didn't come in today. Didn't come in this week at all, actually. How much does he value this company? You could ask him, but you'd have to track down his yacht, so good luck with that—"

"Mr. Amery, I will not take this kind of attitude—"

"Attitude?" asked Joe. He stood up. He was going to explode. He stared at Dorning, whose eyes burned. "You *knew* that I'd be the only one here, didn't you? You waited until everyone else left—"

"I did no such thing—"

"I don't believe you," said Joe. "You've had it in for me ever since that stupid team building exercise."

"Being a part of a team is an important part of our culture—"

Joe laughed at that, a loud laugh, and now everyone who was still there, who wasn't already looking, was looking, staring at the two of them.

"Culture? What culture would that be? To be a helpful little sheep, whenever your boss demands you stay until nine on a holiday weekend?"

"Mr. Amery, this behavior is not acceptable—"

"You're right! Simply unacceptable!" Joe grabbed his backpack, and unzipped it. He pulled open his desk drawer, and grabbed the few belongings inside, and shoved them into his bag. He took the framed picture of him and Helen, folded it up, and put it into his backpack as well. "Would you look at that? Every ounce of me is gone now. How simple was that?"

"Mr. Amery, don't be foolish—"

"Too late for that!" yelled Joe. "Nice knowing you, Steve. Hope those active reports don't keep you here too late. Oh, how foolish of me. Of course they won't, because you'll be gone within a half hour." Joe smiled, his heart burning, breathing fire, and he turned, and he left.

*

"Talk to me, Helen," said Joe. "Say something."

"What am I supposed to say, Joe?"

"Anything."

Helen looked at her hands, clasped, and then down at the floor, and then finally, up at him.

"Do you think it was easy for me to get you that job?"

"No, of course not, but—"

"But what?"

"Dorning waited until everyone else left. He wanted me to stay and work longer. He did it on purpose."

Helen pursed her lips and paused. "So?"

"What do you mean, so? He wanted me to stay until god knows when finishing up everyone's work!"

"Then do it," said Helen, her voice hard.

"No," said Joe. "It's not fair. He didn't like me, and so he targeted me—"

"Do you think you're special, Joe?"

"What kind of question is that?"

"There's a lot of jobs in the world, and in most of them, your boss might be an asshole," said Helen. "Do you think I haven't had asshole bosses?"

"I know you have—"

"Do you think I didn't do the work they asked just because I didn't like them? Because they were unfair?"

"I mean, no, probably not—"

"That's what I mean, Joe. You're not special. Sometimes you have to eat a shit sandwich, no matter how unfair it is."

"Can you take my side, for once?"

"He wasn't asking you to jump off the building, Joe. He was asking you to do your job."

"It wasn't—"

"I don't know how much more of this I can take."

"What?"

Helen stared at him. "I can't do this alone, Joe. I need help."

"I am helping—"

"If you wanted to help, you'd still have a job."

7

Joe texted Wally the next day, but still no answer. He hated using the phone, but he called the next night after work. It rang through to voicemail.

He didn't see him in the cafeteria, and the weekend came, and still nothing. Joe worked on Saturday, but had Sunday off.

By Monday evening, after work, Joe still had heard nothing. No response to the texts, or the calls.

And the rational part of his brain told him to do nothing. To acknowledge that Wally had moved up in the company, and probably didn't have the time or interest in keeping up a friendship with someone who worked in the fulfillment center. That their brief relationship was built only on the fact they had similar jobs.

But Joe thought about the strange questions in the interview. About Wally's preternatural friendliness. Wally wouldn't ignore him, not unless something was wrong.

So Joe waited after his shift was over on Monday evening.

Nile had a security guard at the exit of the facility, but nothing in the parking lot proper. A few other employees gave him a confused gaze as they left for the day, but most ignored him. They all had bigger problems. They all wanted to go home.

So he waited. He would scroll on his phone for a while, glancing up occasionally to see if there was a wave of workers coming, but they were few and far between. He had found Wally's old, small S-10 in the parking lot, and had parked in view of it. Wally wouldn't be able to leave without Joe spotting him.

Joe had to wait for hours, the sun setting. It was dark when he spotted Wally walking to his truck, the lot lit only by a few streetlights. Joe walked up to him as Wally was fishing for his keys.

"Wally," said Joe.

"Jesus!" yelled Wally, looking over at Joe in the dimness. "Is that you, Joe? You scared the shit out of me."

"I'm sorry," said Joe. "I didn't mean to. But I've been worried about you. I texted, left a message, and I hadn't heard anything back—"

"I'm not supposed to talk to you," said Wally, hurriedly, still fishing for his keys. "I'll get in trouble if they see us—"

"I'm sorry," said Joe. "I thought you were in trouble or something—"

Wally found his keys, but then dropped them, and then

kicked them under his truck in his confusion. He took a deep breath and looked at Joe.

"We can't talk here," said Wally. "Follow me to my house? Betsy is probably starving."

"Sure," said Joe.

"Could you—could you grab my keys for me? My knees aren't what they used to be."

*

Wally's house was a little ranch style home even farther out in the suburbs, old, but in decent shape. Betsy jumped up and down excitedly as they went inside, and Wally fed her, dumping a scoop of kibble into a bowl for her. She ate excitedly, and then he let her out into the backyard to do her business. She came back in and laid on her dog bed, next to the couch in the living room.

"My casa is your casa," said Wally. "Help yourself to a drink from the fridge, if you want."

"I'm alright," said Joe. Wally collapsed onto the sofa, the lights still off. The light from the kitchen bled into the rest of the house, enough to see by.

"Sorry about the mess," said Wally. "I've been beat lately. You mind if we keep the light off? My eyes are killing me."

"It's no problem," said Joe. He sat down in the loveseat adjacent to the couch. "There's still enough to see." He said that, but Wally leaned back against the cushion, and he almost vanished. Joe could only see the barest glimpse of the man. He looked tired. "You alright?"

"The new job," said Wally. "It's just about killing me. It's really hard work. I'll make it. I have to."

"I had my interview last week," said Joe. "The interview, Mr. Boggins, said that it was just consulting work. How the hell does consulting work tire you out so badly?"

"It's not—" started Wally. "I can't talk about it. I signed so much paperwork. And all of it amounts to them suing the pants off me if I say a word to anyone."

"Come on, Wally," said Joe. "You can tell me. I won't say anything."

"I can't, Joe," said Wally. "I can't risk losing this job. I've worked so hard, and I'm finally making good money." Wally's voice even sounded strange. Hoarse, in a weird way.

"So, if they offer me the job, I should take it?" asked Joe.

Wally took a breath, and started to say something, but then stopped.

"You can't even recommend me the job?"

"I—" started Wally. "I don't want to give you advice that I end up regretting—" and then his voice disappeared into a coughing fit. Wally leaned forward and coughed hard, his voice ragged, his breath chunky, like he had a terrible cold or bronchitis.

"Jesus, Wally. Let me get you some water," said Joe, who hurried to the kitchen, found a cup, and filled it from the tap. He went back to the living room. The worst of the coughing had subsided, but Wally still was bent over. Joe switched on the lamp nearest the couch, so he could hand him the water. He saw Wally in full light for the first time.

"God, Wally," said Joe. "You look—" But he didn't finish his sentence.

He was going to say *You look like death.*

Wally's skin was sallow, empty of color. His hair seemed a lighter shade of brown, but maybe that was Joe's mind playing tricks on him. Joe wasn't imagining the thin veins visible next to Wally's eyes, or at the edge of his fingernails, thin blue lines. Wally looked twenty years older. It had been a week.

"I didn't want you to see me."

"What are they doing to you?" asked Joe. He handed him the water, and Wally guzzled it down.

"I can't tell—"

"I don't want to hear that bullshit," said Joe. "They're not bugging your house. Tell me what's going on."

Wally drank more water, and then stared at Joe with his weathered eyes.

"It's in the name," said Wally, finally, after a long pause. "Research and development. Well, that's what I'm doing. I'm helping them research and develop."

"Develop what? Radiation poisoning?"

"No," said Wally. "I'm just doing simple tasks. The same ones we do every day, y'know? Picking stuff, moving it between bins, filling orders."

"And that makes you look like a zombie?"

Wally stared at him.

"I'm sorry," said Joe. "I shouldn't have said—"

"It's okay," said Wally. "I know how I look. I haven't been going out at all since—"

"Since what?"

"Since I started getting the shots." Wally looked down as he said it.

"The shots?" asked Joe. "What the fuck does that mean? They're drugging you?"

"Like I said, Joe," said Wally. He looked up again. "Research and development. Part of the deal is getting a shot every day, first thing."

"And you let them?"

"It's part of the job," said Wally. "I—I didn't want to at first. But they said I wouldn't have the job if I wouldn't get the shot. And—and they said my old job wouldn't be waiting for me anymore. So I got the shot."

"What the hell is it?"

"They say it's to improve worker efficiency. As it builds up in the body, it makes you better at the work we do. Repetitive tasks, all that."

"I'm going to be honest, Wally, so please don't take offense," said Joe. "But it looks like it's fucking killing you."

"I know it looks bad," said Wally. "They said it would, to be fair. They warned me. Said the first couple weeks are the hardest on the body. That the immune system doesn't like it at first, has to get used to it. But once it does, it makes you work better."

"But you don't know what it is?"

"They wouldn't tell me exactly," said Wally. "Said it was proprietary. Said if it got out to their competitors, they'd take advantage. So they can't tell me exactly."

"That sounds like bullshit to me."

Wally sighed. "It's the job, Joe," said Wally. "Like I said. I do my time now, and maybe I actually get a retirement. And sure, I look like shit, but in a couple of weeks, it'll fade away, and I'll be working better than I ever did. And I'll finally get paid like I'm worth all that work."

"But everything else is like our normal work? Are you picking actual orders?"

"No," said Wally. "It's all test stuff. Just working in disconnected labs, with different doctors watching. They take notes, and ask questions afterwards."

"What kind of questions?"

"Oh, I don't know," said Wally. "A lot of different ones. Mostly about how I feel doing the tasks. If I feel better or worse, slower or faster. I think they're fine tuning the chemical, or the dose. I don't know."

"Jesus," said Joe. He finally sat back down on the love seat.

Betsy got up, her tail wagging, and hopped up on the couch with Wally, sitting in his lap. Wally stroked her and scratched behind her ears. She fell asleep.

"I know I look terrible," said Wally. "And sure, I feel rough around the edges. But I'm okay. And it hasn't even been a week. They said it takes two weeks or so before the side effects wear off, and your system acclimates. So this is probably the worst of it."

Joe stared at Wally's hands, the veins standing out in his fingers. Joe was going to take the job, he was. But now—

"How's the pay?"

"Better than advertised," said Wally. "Overtime is $100 an hour."

"God almighty," said Joe. "That's crazy."

"Believe me, I'm not doing it for my health," said Wally. "But for that money, I'll take a lot of punishment. Should you take the job, if they offer it? You can do that math."

Joe stared at his own fingers. How much was it worth?

"I was worried about you," said Joe. "You went radio silent all of a sudden. I thought you were in trouble."

"I can't lose the job," said Wally. "I don't have any savings, and no family around. I don't have anywhere else to go, and the mortgage won't pay itself. And Betsy still hasn't found work." She looked up at the sound of her name and then went back to sleep. "You won't tell anyone, will you?"

Joe looked up again, into Wally's sick eyes. "No, I won't say anything. But please, don't ignore me."

"It wasn't the right thing to do, I know, but I was afraid, Joe, that'd you see me like this, and think less of me. After that conversation we had the other night, about doing what you're told and all of that."

"I don't think less of you," said Joe. "But I am still worried."

"Don't be," said Wally. "I'll be okay in a couple weeks, and my bank account will be more than okay. Do you mind heading out? I am just exhausted. I need to catch up on my sleep before work tomorrow."

"No, that's fine," said Joe. "Thanks for not blowing me off." Joe went to leave.

"Hey, Joe," said Wally.

Joe turned back.

"Thanks for caring," said Wally. "I mean it."

"All we have is each other," said Joe. Wally nodded, and Joe left.

Joe got the offer for the promotion the next day.

8

After seeing Wally, and the shape he was in, Joe had told himself there was no way he was accepting the new job. No matter what it paid, it wasn't worth his health.

They were using Wally as a guinea pig, to try some new drug on, and it didn't matter how much they paid, some things weren't worth any amount of money. Nile couldn't buy Joe. They couldn't.

But then HR gave him the offer the next day, first thing. He read through all the paperwork, front to back. And he understood why Wally didn't want to talk.

It did more than threaten the job if he disclosed anything while working for them. If he signed, it would forfeit most of his life if he talked, with Nile gaining all kinds of power over him if he broke the NDA. He didn't know if it would hold up in court, but with Nile's money, they could pay for lawyers for years while he tried to press them. He would lose just as much, if not more, trying to prove it wasn't a legal contract.

But more than that, all his private affirmations of determination and authority felt weak after he saw his pay in writing. It was easy to bullshit about $100/hr overtime with Wally, or anyone else, but when it was right there, in front of him—it wasn't as easy just to say no.

Sure, they would give you some drug that would make you feel miserable and would wreck your body. And maybe you'd have to sign away all your rights.

But the money, the money would be good.

And not just good, but great, six figures, just for being a lab rat and doing work you already were doing.

"I'd like to think it over," said Joe, forcing the words out. He wouldn't decide, not yet.

HR had given him a week to decide, reluctantly, but he hadn't signed anything, so they couldn't deny him the time.

When he got home, he did the math, quietly, in a notebook, and the numbers—they were almost intoxicating.

Six figures. Sure, it was being a lab rat for Nile, but hell, even a year of it would set him and Mom up for some time. He could get her out of the home. Provide her the best care available, all while living with him. No more sleeping on Helen's couch.

He could use the money and go back to school. Learn how to code, and find a cushy desk job, instead of standing on his feet all day.

It was a way out.

He texted Wally.

How you feeling today?

Wally had promised to answer his texts, and he was true to his word, replying a few minutes later.

Still beat up, but thinking I'm seeing the light at the end of tunnel.

He had told himself he wouldn't do it, he couldn't. It was about the principle of the thing. He couldn't be bought or sold.

And that's what he told himself as he picked orders the next day, his feet dully thudding in his sneakers. He wasn't taking ibuprofen any more, it didn't hurt that much, but it still hurt, would always hurt, especially at the end of the day.

In the silence, as he moved items from one plastic bin to another, he had a lot of time to think. And over time, that resolve to not sell out or give in to Nile's offer eroded.

Within a month, he'd be out of debt.

Within two, he'd have an apartment, and his mom living with him.

Within three, he'd have a new car. One that wouldn't break down in the parking lot, or on the side of the road.

Within six months, he'd have savings. Real savings. A real safety net.

And when he got home every night, he would text Wally.

How you doing, buddy?

And Wally would answer.

Hanging in there. Aches all over. But still standing.

Wally stayed in touch with him, and his answers kept Joe from giving in. Because as the week passed, Wally's answers didn't change that much.

How you doing? Joe would ask.

Wally would answer.

Still hurting, but I'm alright.

Hoping it wears off soon, but I'll make it.

It's hard. I can handle it.

It was getting close to the deadline. Joe would have to give them an answer soon, within two days. He had told himself, if Wally was still feeling bad, that he would tell them no. No matter how much money it was, if he felt miserable and sick, it wasn't worth six figures. No amount of money was worth it.

He *would* tell them no.

But there was a part of him, a desperate part, that hoped Wally would answer back with *Feeling better.* Or *My body is getting used to it.*

So when Joe texted him, he hoped that's what he'd get back. Something that would give him an excuse to say yes. An opportunity to keep that money, and that pay, even if it was miserable.

Your job already is miserable. What's a little bit more?

But Wally's answer never came. Joe gave him more time. Maybe he had to run errands, or he didn't notice his text. But all the others had come quickly, and had been at about the same time.

He waited an hour, and there was a sick feeling in the pit of his stomach, and he felt stupid, but he called. He'd rather feel stupid, but know that Wally was okay.

But there was no answer. Joe left a voicemail.

He kept his phone close all night, but still no answer, and no response to his texts.

Something was wrong, he knew it. But what was it? Had they found out Wally had said something? Or did Wally suspect they did? Was Wally sick, too sick to respond?

Joe tossed and turned all night, and showed up to work a few minutes early. Because he'd been doing more than just texting Wally. He'd also been keeping an eye on Wally's old truck. Every morning it had sat in the same place in the parking lot.

Today, it wasn't there.

Joe didn't know what that meant. There was no answer that morning either. But his gut told him something was wrong.

He had to work, though, the whole day ahead of him. Maybe it was nothing. Maybe there was a good reason Wally wasn't answering.

Joe worked, trying to keep his mind off of Wally, off of his promotion. But the empty day demanded his mind fill the void, and it did with anxiety about Wally. What if Wally was sick? What if he had to go to the doctor, and Nile was trying to cover it up?

And then he realized that he knew someone who would know.

Anna, the scientist. If he could find her at lunch, maybe he could get an answer from her. At least a clue.

But he'd have to have the same lunch as her.

When did he see her before? It was the 12:30 lunch shift. She had been there then, already, sitting. He'd take the same shift today, and talk to her.

The lunch break came slowly, with Joe's mind casting about in chaos the entire time, as well as his stomach growling. Would she be there? He didn't know, but it was worth a shot.

Joe clocked out and practically ran to the cafeteria, grabbing his lunch from a fridge and dodging the groups waiting in line at the array of vending machines. He scanned the people sitting at tables, mostly the rank and file who worked with him. Very few lab coats, and none of them women. Damn it, a dead end.

But then his eye caught blonde hair deep in the corner, her back to him, wearing a lab coat. Had to be her.

"Anna?" asked Joe, hurrying to her. She glanced back, and he was proven correct. He didn't ask to sit next to her, taking the seat.

"Uh, hi," she said with a small smile. She had the same salad in front of her as the other day.

"You eat the same thing every day?"

"Not every day," said Anna.

"Sorry if I said something wrong the other day."

"The other day?"

"Yeah, when we met," said Joe. "You left in a hurry. I assumed I said something wrong."

"No, it's not that," said Anna. "It's—it's complicated. But it's not your fault."

"Everything going alright over in your neck of the woods?"

"As well as it can," said Anna. Joe needed an answer about Wally. But how to get it?

"Still can't divulge any state secrets?"

"Uh, sorry, no," said Anna. Joe leaned in a little to her and lowered his voice.

"They offered me a job over there, you know."

"They did?"

"Yeah," said Joe. "I've been thinking about it. I only have a couple more days to mull it over. Huge pay increase. Hard to say no."

Anna glanced at him quickly, and then back down at her salad.

"We'd be coworkers, right? You think I should take the job?"

Anna coughed then, spitting out pieces of lettuce into her bowl. She coughed hard and reached for her water, taking a drink.

"You alright?"

"Y—yeah," forced out Anna. "I'm sorry about that." She swallowed more water.

"Is that a no?"

"I—I can't tell you what to do," said Anna. "But—" She paused, and looked back down at her salad, and took a breath. Joe looked in her eyes. She was choosing her words. "I think you can do better."

What does that mean?

He lowered his voice even more.

"Anna," said Joe. "What's going on over there? Have you seen my friend Wally? Is he okay?"

Anna looked at him again, with alarm in her eyes, and then looked back at her half eaten salad.

"I can't say anything—" she said. "What's your number?"

"What?" asked Joe.

"Your cell," she said, quietly, without looking at him.

"555-555-7431. But I don't have it, we can't bring our phones in—"

She pulled out her phone. She didn't work in the fulfillment center. The same rules didn't apply. Her fingers danced across the screen quickly.

"Check your phone when you leave," she said. "I have to go. We can't talk. We can't."

And then she left, throwing what remained of her salad away.

"Fuck," said Joe, under his breath. He wouldn't see his phone again for five hours. And now he had six minutes to eat. He devoured his sandwich and crackers, and hurried back to his workstation.

The rest of the day crawled, his mind focused only on what Anna texted him. She was paranoid. She didn't want him to take the job. What the hell was going on with R&D? Where was Wally?

He picked orders, going as fast as he could, trying to stay busy, but every minute moved at a snail's pace.

Finally, he got out of work, and did everything but sprint to his car, where his phone waited for him in the glove box. He opened it frantically. He had a lot of notifications waiting for him, but he thumbed through them quickly, looking for Anna's text.

He found it, a message from an unknown number. It was short, only four words.

Please check on Betsy.

Joe's heart froze.

The memory of Betsy licking his hand. Of sleeping on Wally's ailing lap. Anna knew about Betsy. Why would he need to check—

Terrible thoughts flew through Joe's mind, and he turned the key in his car, and tried not to crash on the way to Wally's house.

He got there in fifteen minutes. Wally's truck wasn't there either. It was missing entirely.

What the hell was going on?

He parked in the driveway. The lights were off inside. He

tried the front door, and it was locked. He looked around the front stoop.

He lifted the mat. No key. A flower pot near the door. Nothing, either.

Damn it.

Well, he would break in if he had to. He glanced back at the surrounding neighborhood. There was no movement. Two bricks sat next to the other side of the door, and he picked one up, only to reveal a key beneath it. He grabbed the key and opened the door.

Betsy was there, on top of him, jumping up and down, frantically happy to see someone.

"Hey girl," said Joe, petting and hugging her. She licked his face. And then he smelled it. The house stunk. Smelled like urine and dog poop. He looked down at Betsy, who stared up at him, her tail wagging. "How long have you been alone, girl?"

He went to the back door and opened it, and she sprinted into Wally's small backyard, immediately peeing, and then pooping, and then sprinted right back. Joe went to her food and water bowls. The water bowl had a mere sliver of water in it, and her food bowl was empty. He fed her, and while Betsy ate, he cleaned and filled her water. She ate and then drank greedily.

"You must be starving," said Joe. There was a deep ache building in his gut. Joe walked through the house, looking for any sign of any clues for Wally's whereabouts. There was nothing, except for a sink filled with dishes and trash that needed to be taken out.

The only thing that was clear was that Wally hadn't been here for over a day, and his truck was gone. He wouldn't leave Betsy like this, not of his own volition.

Nile had done something with him.

9

Joe waited in the Walmart parking lot. Betsy sat in the back seat, softly slumbering, her tongue hanging out.

Where the hell was she?

After searching Wally's house, he texted Anna. They needed to talk. She had agreed, eventually, to meet at the Walmart two towns over. It was public, but isolated, and far enough away from Nile for her to feel comfortable.

A white crossover SUV parked nearby, and a cloaked figure got out, hustling over to Joe's small car. The figure climbed in and shut the door, pulling down her hood to reveal Anna.

Betsy saw her climb in and stood up, sticking her head up between the seats to smell and then lick her face. Anna smiled and pet the dog, the smile disappearing after a second.

"This must be Betsy," said Anna.

"Yeah," said Joe. "She was hungry."

Silence hung between them.

"Where's Wally, Anna?" asked Joe, finally.

Anna absentmindedly pet Betsy. "I don't know."

"You don't know?" asked Joe. "Or you won't tell me?"

"I don't know where he is," said Anna. "That's the truth."

"Then why did you tell me to check on Betsy?" asked Joe. "How did you know about Betsy at all?"

"Wally told me about her," said Anna. "While we worked together. He loved her, it was clear. Loved talking about her. I wanted to make sure she was okay."

"But you don't know where Wally is?" asked Joe. "What the hell is going on?"

Anna was silent. Joe was about to ask again when she spoke up.

"They took Wally to processing."

"What the hell does that mean?" asked Joe.

"I don't know," said Anna, and she cried, burying her face in her hands. She sobbed, and Joe didn't know what to do. He finally flipped open the center console and dug around until he found a thin stack of brown fast food napkins. He handed them to her, and she used one to wipe away her tears.

"I—" Joe started. "I just want to know what happened to my friend."

"I'm not lying," said Anna. "I don't know where Wally is. I only suspect."

"What do you suspect?"

Another long silence, and then Anna stared at him. "I

suspect he's dead."

Joe's heart burned cold. He reached back to pet Betsy.

"What do you know?" asked Joe. "And please, just straight answers."

"I don't mean to lie," said Anna. "But they watch so closely. Everything is monitored. And they keep us all separated. No one has complete information. They tell us it's to protect us. But it's just to keep us in the dark, so we'll keep working on their dirty secrets."

"Anna—"

"I started a year ago," said Anna. "I wasn't lying, about that. I moved here, to work for Nile."

"What do you do?"

"I'm a behaviorist," said Anna. "Social psychology. My doctorate was on efficiency in the workplace."

"That's what Boggins told me you were working on during my interview," said Joe. "Efficiency."

"Nile is leagues ahead of everyone else," said Anna. "It's partially why they've done so well. They exploit all the shortcuts people make in their minds to make their employees' work mean more, and go further. It's really incredible, and it was one of the main features of my studies. It's probably why they hired me, to be honest. If I had known then, what I know now—"

"You worked with Wally?"

"Yeah," said Anna. "I work with everyone when they first come into R&D. They need me to establish a baseline. That's what they call it. They call it a baseline."

"A baseline of what?"

"Of what they can do," said Anna. "I was stupid. So stupid. I had seen the news. Everyone has, you'd have to be blind not to see it. About Nile, and how they punish their workers. How they overwork them, take advantage of them. And not even just their warehouse workers, but their white-collar people too. But I thought, no, *I'll* be different. *I'll* be the exception. And even if it's hard, I only have to deal with it for a few years. If I don't like it, I can quit, and I'll have built up a nest egg, and I'll have some clout—" She shook her head. "So stupid. I'm no different from everyone else."

"Why do they need a baseline?"

"I had big ideas," said Anna. "But they're having me do the simplest things. Any grad student could handle this. Don't know why they're paying me so much to do so little." She paused. "The baseline is how well all the workers do the normal stuff. Pick orders, sort them, ship them. Everything they already do in the fulfillment center. So that as they progress through the program, they can measure their efficiency at the end versus how they were at the beginning."

"Wally told me—told me they were giving him some chemical," said Joe. "Every day, they were injecting him with something. He looked terrible. It looked like it was killing him."

"I'm not even supposed to know about it," said Anna. "Anything not directly involved in your own work, you're in the dark. But it's impossible not to notice. The track marks, the way the people would get more and more sluggish, day by day. The bags under their eyes. Their skin changing color. Impossible not to see. And all of them talked about it. They weren't supposed to, but that didn't stop them."

"What is it?"

"I don't know," said Anna. "They keep me in the dark

about it. My bosses have never told me, and I've never asked. But whatever it is—"

"It's killing them."

Anna exhaled. "Maybe they're still alive," said Anna. "Maybe. The R&D facility is huge, and there's technically room in there to house everyone. Maybe that's why they don't go home, why security moves their vehicles—"

"Is that why Wally's truck wasn't at work?"

"I think so," said Anna. "It's my guess. Nile has so much property. There's plenty of places for them to store the vehicles."

"Why would they give them that stuff if it kills them?"

"That's what I can't figure out," said Anna.

"They told Wally that it would wear off," said Joe. "That his body would get used to it. Is there a chance it's true?"

"I don't know," said Anna. "I *never* see them again. Could they be doing better? It's possible, sure. But why would Nile make them disappear?"

"Boggins asked me a bunch of personal questions," said Joe. "Stuff that didn't make sense, about my health history, and my family. But if they were planning on me to disappear, they would need to know if anyone would notice. Wally doesn't have any family. Betsy is his only dependent."

Betsy perked up at her name and poked her head forward again.

"Will you be able to take care of her?" asked Anna.

"I think so," said Joe. "My roommate, Helen—she loves corgis. I think she'll like her. But, we have to do something. I at least have to find out what happened to Wally. I can't just abandon him. Not without knowing."

"I can't do anything."

"It's just a job."

"I would have quit already if that was true," said Anna. "I don't—I don't know what will happen if I leave."

"What, like they'll come after you?"

"I'm afraid," said Anna. "Maybe it's nothing. But if I said anything to the press—they know where I live. They know everything about me. What's protecting me?"

"Can you get me into R&D?"

"My hands are tied," said Anna. "I could swipe us into the building, sure, but they'd notice you were there, and I'd be fired. Fired if I'm lucky. If they can make all those people disappear, why couldn't they make me disappear? Or you?"

"There's no way without being tracked?"

"Not with my card. They track everywhere I go in the building, but there are other ways. Who knows if they'd work though—"

"What are they?"

"Well, there's a ton of security at the fulfillment center, right?"

"Yeah," said Joe. "We have to go through a metal detector on the way in and out."

"Doesn't exist in R&D," said Anna. "There's guards, and cameras at the entrances, but not anywhere else. They want nothing filmed. They're desperately afraid of leaks."

"So if I can get in, no one will see me?"

"Right," said Anna. "And they can't track your movement without a card."

"But how do I get anywhere if all the doors are keyed to access cards?"

"There are guards at the entrance," said Anna. "But they're lazy. We get a lot of deliveries. A lot of them. Probably thirty a day. And security is supposed to take the packages and then hand them off to the right people."

"But they don't?"

"No," said Anna. "They would be delivering packages all day. So they give the delivery guys access cards, so they can deliver the packages to the interior labs."

"I'm guessing it's limited access, though?"

"That's what they say," said Anna. "But I've heard security talk, when they didn't know I could hear them. And they tell the delivery guys to only deliver to select labs, where there's nothing sensitive. But the cards are coded to open any door. The delivery guys have never tested it, because why would they? They want to deliver their packages and get out. But if you got a hold of one of those cards, you could go anywhere."

"So, pretend I have a delivery, and get one of the cards."

"Yeah," said Anna. "But if they catch you in the wrong lab—"

"There'd be trouble," said Joe. "Yeah, I figure that. I won't get caught."

"Are you sure it's worth this?" asked Anna. She took a deep breath. "It's easier to just forget this all happened."

Joe looked back at Betsy, whose tail started wagging.

"Doesn't work that way for me," said Joe. "When should I go in?"

"Probably late would be best," said Anna. "Overnight, if possible."

"Won't they be suspicious, if I have a delivery at midnight?" asked Joe.

"Just tell them you're taking extra work, to make rent," said Anna. "They won't blink an eye."

10

He hit the buzzer outside the double metal doors. A camera glared down on him, and he glanced at it and then looked away. Butterflies danced in his stomach. He hadn't wasted any time. He had dropped Betsy off at Helen's, and then came straight here. Helen had been hesitant for a moment, but then Betsy gave her the puppy dog eyes, and she had agreed to keep her.

"Yes?" said the intercom.

"Delivery," said Joe. "Development lab." He said what Anna told him to say. He didn't know what the development lab was, but she said it would get him in.

The buzzer sounded, and Joe pulled the door open. Two guards sat at the front desk. One stared at his phone without looking up. The other eyed him.

"You been here before?" he asked. He wore a black shirt and pants, with a ballistics vest over top of it. A pistol was strapped to his belt. Joe tried not to stare at it.

"No," said Joe.

"Kinda late, isn't it?" he asked.

"Gotta make money, man," said Joe. "Packages don't care when they get delivered."

"Fair," said the guard. He pulled open a drawer and pulled out something, sliding it on the counter to Joe. A thin white piece of plastic. A key card. "This will get you to the development lab. Go nowhere else. No diversions."

"How do I get there?"

"It's easy," said the guard. He pointed down the hall. "Through the door, then your second right into another hallway. Development lab will be your third door on your right. There'll be a sign. Run the card over the sensor and wait for the green light. Drop the package off on the big table near the entrance. Understood?"

"Got it," said Joe. He went to go.

"Wait a second," said the guard. "You need to sign in. Name, company, package number." He slid a clipboard over to Joe.

Joe took the pen and wrote "Steve Sanders" down quickly, and then copied one of the company names from higher in the list, Dawson Logistics, and cobbled together a fake number that seemed to match the other numbers already listed. He handed it back, nodded to the guard, and walked toward the first door without waiting for the guard to examine his credentials.

Confidence, Joe. Project confidence. You're just here to deliver a package.

The guard didn't stop him again. Joe waved the card past the scanner and the light lit green and he pulled open the heavy door and went through. The subtle ache in his guts eased a little, with a door between him and the guards, the lock clicking shut behind him. There was a small window in the door, and he couldn't dally here, just in case they looked.

He glanced around, and looked at the other doors, but the hallway was nondescript, with carpeted floors, and landscapes hanging on the walls. It was nondescript on purpose. Just another Nile office. Joe glanced down the hall, and saw a sign for the executive suites at the far end. He didn't have time. Joe needed to hustle now if he wanted any amount of time to explore the rest of the facility. He didn't know if the guards would keep a close eye on him, and how long he had, but the clock ticked inside his head. If he got caught snooping, they'd probably just kick him out, but he didn't want to test his theory.

He waved his card in front of the second door on his right, with a sign that read "Testing Labs", and moved through as soon as the light lit up green.

As the door clicked shut behind him, Joe noticed the immediate change in the decor. No more landscapes or decorations of any kind. The floors were tile here, the walls a dull green. The hallway was long, heading down at least a hundred yards, and then hitting a T junction.

Joe hurried down to the third door, with a sign that read "Development Lab". Anna had told him this was where the employees went after their time with her was done. Where they went before they disappeared from the outside world. Development Lab seemed so innocuous. Joe looked back, on reflex, but he was still alone. The guards weren't following him. They were sitting at their station, staring at their phones. Maybe if he wasn't back in twenty minutes they'd come and check on him.

He scanned his card and pushed through the door, into the Development Labs.

He hadn't known what to expect. He'd never seen the inside of a lab, and the most white-collar job he had worked was data entry with Helen's company, and he had sat in a cubicle farm.

This didn't look that much different. Well, it looked more expensive.

The office was big and open, with an array of desks in front of him, with bigger offices ringing the walls. He spotted the big table the guard had told him about, and he dropped off the package he carried, a medium-sized box that was filled with nothing but packing peanuts. It was addressed to no one in particular, and hopefully would be opened and then forgotten.

He glanced at the time, and gave himself ten minutes. It was the absolute longest he could stay in there, and then he would head back out.

Joe looked around the office area. A lot of monitors, a few with log-in screens displayed, the rest turned off. He was sure they would contain all kinds of information, but there was no way he'd be able to get into them, not in ten minutes. Maybe if he had more time, but that wouldn't be for tonight. He would need to find hard evidence. There was a door at the far end of the room, past the maze of desks, and he hurried to it. The door was unlabeled, but it required no scan to get in, and he pulled the door and went through.

The smell was the first thing that hit him. It was a strong

odor, of antiseptic and bleach. The smell of something being disinfected, of a doctor's office, of a hospital—

Of a morgue.

But he was only in a hallway, a short one at that, compared to the one he just left. There were only two doors in it. Both had signs on them.

One read "Live Application".

The other read "Post Application".

What the hell does that mean?

The doors looked identical in all other ways. There was no evidence.

Joe didn't have all day to decide, and went in the first door, "Live Application".

The room smelled like chemicals, like a swimming pool, but ten thousand times more potent, the scent of toxicity and poison. It was tile and stainless steel, massive, the side wall covered in computers and machinery, intermixed with vials of liquids of all colors and sizes. The largest was huge, an immense container. There was sluiced grating in the floor, the grating covering a channel that disappeared into the wall.

But that wasn't the strangest thing. The strangest thing was the workstations.

Joe recognized them. They were identical to the fulfillment center workstations, where employees would unload incoming shipments, pick orders like Joe did, and then box them for shipping out to customers. There was one workstation for each of the three jobs. But they weren't identical to the workstations out in the center, not exactly.

Thick metal bars surrounded each of them, with a heavy door embedded in the middle of the bars, like a jail cell.

Each of the workstations was completely enclosed.

What the fuck?

Were they imprisoning them? Anna had mentioned setting a baseline for their work in the fulfillment center, but why on Earth were their bars here? They were getting paid. Why would they have to be imprisoned?

The slim shred of hope that Joe had about finding Wally slowly dwindled. What the fuck was Nile doing here? His eyes passed over the wall of computers and chemicals. They were injecting the workers with something, and then making them do their jobs?

There was still something missing. Joe didn't have the full picture. And there was no sign of the lost people here, of Wally himself. There was nothing else in the room.

Joe looked at his watch. He had little time left, only a few minutes. Joe hoped there were answers in the other lab. He hoped Wally was there.

He left Live Application, and stood in front of Post Application. He took a deep breath.

Wally is inside this door. He has to be. You'll find your answer and get him out and reunite him with Betsy.

Joe opened the door and went inside. He was greeted by utter darkness.

All the other offices and labs had automatic lighting, with overhead lights kicking on whenever they sensed movement.

But not here. Joe stood in the dark, waiting for the lights to turn on, but nothing happened.

In those moments he waited, the smell of the room hit him, and hit him hard, harder than anywhere else.

The stench nearly knocked him over.

This wasn't the smell of disinfectant, or bleach, or the chemical odor of chlorine that was in the other lab.

This was the smell of rot.

The scent of decay, of death, of bloat, of blood, and shit, and horror.

Joe coughed, doubling over, unable to stop himself. He covered his mouth and nose with his shirt, and took short, shallow breaths.

What the fuck, what the fuck—

The light still hadn't kicked on, and he needed his phone, he could use the flashlight, and find the light switch.

That's when he heard the sounds.

They were quiet at first, easily missed in his own panic in the dark. But now he heard them, and he froze.

A soft shuffling was all he heard at first. But then he heard the voices. Only one at first, but the longer he stayed still and silent, he heard more of them.

It was unintelligible, but in the intervening seconds, his ears picked out words from the groans, moans, and murmurs.

"—Ooorder Nnnumber—"

"—Booox sizee ffourr—"

"—Tape dowwwn next—"

Tears welled in the corners of his eyes, and Joe blinked them away, reaching for his phone. He needed the light, needed to see what was going on—were the noises getting closer to him?

Something was wrong, something was wrong, and Joe scrambled for his phone, it was in his pocket, but his damn hand was getting caught, and then he finally pulled it out, and tapped the flashlight on.

He cast about in the darkness with the small light of his phone and he found the door he came in, and looked nearby.

Ignore the noises, ignore the noises

And then he found the light switch, and he flicked it on, there were four of them, and he flicked them all on.

The overhead lights came on, and Joe saw.

Saw the source of the sounds, of the smells.

The space was big, bigger even than the other lab. The walls were lined with cells, with bars and doors much like the ones that contained the workstations next door. But there were no workstations inside the cells.

There were only people.

Some cells contained only a couple of people. Others contained almost ten, crammed in close together.

Oh god, oh god—

They had them imprisoned, all of them.

"I'll get you out—" started Joe. "I'll get you all out of here, just give me a second, I'll find a release lever, or something—" His eyes darted around the room. The middle of the room had some stainless steel tables, and some matching cabinets nearby, but he couldn't see a way to release the cell doors—

And then he saw the panel on the far wall, and he hurried to it. They couldn't get away with this, he couldn't allow it, the worry of being caught disappeared, replaced with anger, all of them, together, they could storm the security guards—

He hurried to the panel, but then his eyes glanced over at a cell, and he saw Wally. Joe paused.

"Wally? Wally, is that you?" he asked, approaching the cell. Wally was stuck in there with three other people, two men and a woman. They all were vacant eyed, and stared at the wall, or the floor, their hands absently moving through the air.

"Wally?" Joe asked again, but Wally didn't respond. His hands moved, grabbing and moving nothing. "Wally, snap out of it, what have they done to you—"

But then Joe realized. He hadn't pieced it all together. The stench was awful, of course it was. Keeping so many people, so close together, without showers, with no bathrooms, the smell *would* be bad.

But that didn't explain why no one responded to him. No one was talking. Why Wally wouldn't look him in the eye.

He looked at Wally, in the shadows of his cell. His skin was sallow, worse than it was before. Dark red veins streaked through his eyes. His left arm was a nightmare, pus leaking from track marks at his inner elbow.

All those things could be explained.

But Joe couldn't explain why Wally wasn't breathing. His chest did not rise and fall.

No matter what condition Wally was in, he would have to breathe.

Tears fell from Joe's eyes, as he stared at Wally, waiting for him to take a breath. It didn't happen, and the terrible ache in the pit of his stomach exploded in agony.

They had killed Wally, and now, he was a fucking zombie.

11

What the fuck!

Wally didn't breathe, they killed him, those fuckers, but he was alive, he was moving.

Joe looked around the room, at all the people, all of them undead. Zombies, motherfucking zombies—

"This can't be real, there has to be an explanation—"

But none of the zombies answered. They stared blankly ahead, some moving their arms absentmindedly—

What were they doing?

The pieces of the puzzle moved in Joe's mind, still in chaos. *This is impossible, this is impossible—*

But every single one of these people—

They're not people anymore, they're dead, they're DEAD—

Why would Nile do this? This is murder, people would

discover, they would have to pay for it—

Joe looked from cell to cell, trying to find any sign of life, but there were no beds in the cells, no bathrooms, no food, no water, because they didn't *need* any of that anymore. They would persist as long as their bodies held together.

He stared at one creature, and watched what it did, watched its hands move, waving in the air, reaching out to nothing, and putting the nothing down and—

And then the puzzle pieces fit together, latched onto each other inside his mind. He recognized those movements, now. Divorced from context, it had taken him a few minutes to understand. But he knew those motions. He had done them himself, hundreds of times already, in just the brief time he had worked for Nile. If he worked there long enough, that number would creep up into the thousands, the tens of thousands.

The zombie was picking orders.

Not literally, but it was following those same motions. Even with no workstation, it was doing what it did in life, what it had been trained to do with mindless efficiency. What Joe had been trained to do, and did.

It all made sense. Anna had been testing the employees when they switched over to R&D. A baseline, she had said. A baseline against what?

A baseline against *this*.

Nile needed to know how well the living employee would do against the undead one. The caged workstations made sense now. Joe pictured it in his mind. A team of people grabbing one zombie out of its cell, and leading it over to one of the caged workstations. They would present it with the same situation that it had been tested as a human. It knew only what it knew in life. The scientists would take notes, and they would coldly compare the skills of the undead worker versus their capabilities as the living version of themselves.

Joe stared at the creature, mindlessly working, its hands moving and picking packages without even realizing what it was doing. It was horrific. It was once a woman. Flesh had rotted off its face, the muscle and sinew poking through, and even after being exposed for several minutes, the smell nearly overwhelmed Joe. This was a monster, an abomination. The mere sight of the undead provoked a rage, an anger, a deep burning desire to destroy this unholy nightmare, an affront against humanity. Joe was seized by the need to open the gate, to crush this thing into nothing, until it was truly dead, to end whatever existence it had left. It and its brethren were things that should not be.

His chest burned with rage, but he knew it shouldn't be at these creatures, no. They were all innocent, all victims. They had been promised a way out of their lives, a path to success. And all of them had the same thoughts Joe had. All of them had worked for Nile and had gone through the same treatment working in the fulfillment center. Of long hours, of mandatory overtime, of rushing through lunch to avoid being yelled at by their boss. They had endured all of it to pay their rent, to feed their children.

And I'm sure they all had their doubts. All had the thought that it was too good to be true. But then they saw the dollar amount. And they had dreamed, just like Joe had dreamed. Of a better life, of a life they had been promised as children, and here it was, and all they had to do was reach out and grab it.

And then Nile had injected them with death and venom and had killed them. And whatever Nile injected them with—it didn't just kill them. It brought them back, as whatever the hell monsters they were, not living or dying. As zombies.

Joe looked at them, all of them, and he saw only horror. The utter corruption and abuse filed into cages to slowly rot while Nile worked their science. Joe only saw the disgusting callous abuse of humanity.

But he knew that wasn't what Nile saw when they looked into these cages.

They didn't see horror or murder or abuse or torture.

They saw the perfect worker.

Because what else could these things be?

They didn't need to eat or drink. They would never sleep. They wouldn't rankle against their boss, or take a long bathroom break. They wouldn't steal, or show up late. They wouldn't take a vacation. They wouldn't feel guilty about leaving their kid at home, or needing to take a Friday off to go to the doctor.

A slave was too good a term for what they were, because a slave still had needs.

These creatures would serve until their bodies rotted, until there was nothing left, until whatever chemical will that reanimated them wore off.

They wouldn't draw a paycheck. The only cost was human, and Nile would pay that gladly.

How did they think they would get away with us?

Dozens of people murdered.

But then Joe remembered the questions. About family. About relatives. Joe looked around the room and walked back to Wally's cage, where he stood in the same spot. Wally only had Betsy, but Betsy wouldn't call the police or file a missing persons report.

All of these people were hired for the same reason. All of them had minimal family. They had no support system, no one to care if they went missing.

Nile knew that and had picked them for that very reason.

Joe stared at what once was Wally.

"I'll take care of Betsy, don't you worry," said Joe. "And I'll make them pay. I swear."

Wally turned then, and looked at Joe for the first time. There was a spark of hope in Joe's heart, just for a moment. Maybe there was something still human in him, after all. Maybe they could salvage it. Maybe he could bring Wally back, maybe this wasn't the end—

And then Wally lunged, sprinting at the cage walls, his arms outstretched, a deep growl echoing out of Wally's empty chest. Joe fell backward out of surprise, and it might have saved his life.

Wally hit the iron bars with incredible force, his skull ringing off the hard metal. His arms went out through the cage and reached for Joe, grasping at the air, and Wally's teeth clacked together, over and over again.

CLACK

CLACK

CLACK

Wally's actions had attracted the slow attention of all the others, and they all looked at him, and one by one they followed Wally's lead, all of them pressing forward, to the front walls of their cage, growling, yelling, moaning in righteous anger. They reached for him, the sound of their gnashing teeth filling the room.

They would kill him if they could. With the same mindless efficiency they worked to pick orders, they would pick apart Joe's body. Whatever had given them unnatural life had given them a dark rage.

He couldn't let them out. They'd tear him apart. Joe would have to leave and bring down the hammer on Nile from without. Reveal the truth to whoever would care, and—

He heard the door open, and he looked to see the guards pushing through.

Oh shit

Joe only had a second to hide.

"What the fuck is the commotion in here?" asked one of the voices.

Joe spider crawled behind a cabinet in the middle of the room.

"You leave the light on in here on your last patrol?" asked the other guard.

"I honestly don't remember," said the other voice. Joe heard the door close and footsteps as the two guards moved into the room. The cabinet door was behind him. He slowly opened it, hoping there was room for him in there, it was a big cabinet—there was a chance—

Their footsteps came closer.

"They sure are worked up about something," said the first guard.

Joe leaned inside the cabinet, there was room in there, if barely, he hoped it was quiet, but the zombies were making some noise, maybe they would hide his. He pulled his legs into the space, and he felt something inside shift, and he grabbed and clutched it, the cold metal shape in his arms. They'd see him in a second, and he pulled the cabinet shut, leaving him in the dark.

"They're mindless," said the second guard, his voice muffled. "They're calm one second, and then angry the next. Who gives a shit? They'll be gone in a month. Rotted away."

The two guards had passed the cabinet. They were right outside, and Joe hoped they didn't notice a difference.

"It's kinda fucked up," said the second guard, softer.

"What did I tell you?"

"I know, I know."

"They knew the risks when they signed the paperwork. They saw the pay and took their chances."

"I mean, yeah, if they read all the paperwork—"

"It's not your fault if they're too stupid to read," said the first guard. "It's too late now, anyway. They're angry about nothing. They'll calm down in the dark."

The two guards left, the light turning off. Joe waited another thirty seconds and then got out of the cabinet. He still heard the zombies groaning in the dark, but the guard was right. They were quieting down.

His heart raced. He needed to get out. He'd been gone too long, and they'd be suspicious. Still, there was only one way out.

He used his phone to find his way to the door and poked his head out. No guards. He rushed, peeking out every door beforehand, making sure security wasn't waiting for him, but they were nowhere to be found. Who knew how big the facility was, how far back the other labs went. They could be patrolling everything.

He hurried back to the front entrance, which was empty,

and he took the opportunity, dropping off the key card and getting out. He didn't stop until he was back inside his car, and immediately headed to Helen's.

His eyes were in the rear-view mirror the whole time, looking for someone following him. But no one did.

12

"Do you have to go?"

Joe looked up at his mom, already in her uniform. She looked down on him, her face still. She took a breath.

"I'm sorry, honey," she said. "But I have to go in."

"But it's Christmas—"

"I know," she said. "I don't want to do it, but I need to take the shift. You play your game, okay? I'll be back before you know it."

Joe held the controller. He looked away from her, finally. "I will."

"I love you," she said.

"I love you, too."

And then she was gone, the door closing and locking, the sound of their tiny car starting up and driving away.

Joe listened to it go, and then unpaused his game. He had asked for it for Christmas, and had unwrapped it only hours ago, and had jumped at the chance to play it.

And now he had all day.

He played, throwing himself into the game, letting it wash over him. He'd never seen anything like this. The world, the guns—it was all so much, and the time melted away as he spent time inside of it.

But he still glanced backwards. Dad had used to watch him play, before the accident. He liked to think that he still did, somehow.

Mom had done it too, after. When she was home, at least. She'd sit, and read, and watch him as he played. When she wasn't working.

The hours passed. Joe looked away from the screen and realized it was dark. He paused the game, and the sound disappeared, and the apartment was silent.

Joe stood, stretching his legs, and walked around. He looked into the quiet rooms. The laundry room, the kitchen, his bedroom, his mother's room, and the bathroom.

He didn't know why he wandered, but he suddenly desperately missed his mother. He wanted her there, wanted her behind him, wanted her presence on the couch, just to sit and read idly while he played, knowing she was there.

Joe returned to the living room and stared at the screen. He had asked for the game for Christmas, had asked for it for months, ever since it came out, and his mom said not to hold his breath. But then Christmas came, and the game was there, and he had hugged her so hard—

But it was why she was working, he knew. An extra couple shifts to pick up the slack. To get him a game, or a book he wanted, or to pad out their grocery store trips—

Joe turned off the game and went to the closet. He stood on his tiptoes, but he wasn't tall enough, and so he got the stepladder, and used it to get to the higher shelves. It was where they kept the stash of art supplies, of markers, and glue, and construction paper, and a dozen other odds and ends he had mostly grown out of playing with.

He grabbed everything and moved it to the kitchen table. He'd make her something.

But what to make?

A card? No, he'd gotten her a card. Gotten her a card and a candle, and she had smiled when she opened them. He could have gotten her anything, and she would have smiled. She never told him what she wanted.

Joe looked around the room, and finally his eyes settled on the Christmas tree set up in the corner.

Of course!

He got to work. He grabbed scissors, and the colored pencils, and the construction paper, and hunted around the apartment for the other miscellaneous things he needed, and crafted his mom's gift.

Joe cut and drew. He didn't have everything he wanted, but he'd make due, and he looked at the clock, and it was past his bedtime, but he'd finish it before she got home, he had to, and he leaned his head down on the table, just for a second, just needed to close his eyes—

"Honey?" asked his mom, and Joe opened his eyes to see her standing over him. "Are you okay?"

"You're home," he said, blinking away the sleep.

"You fell asleep," she said. "Let's get you to bed. What were you doing?" She scanned the kitchen table, covered in scraps and supplies. His arms partially covered his creation. She reached out and grabbed it.

"Wait, it's not done yet—" he started, but she already had it, looking at it, turning it over in her hands.

"Oh, Joe," she said.

"It's an ornament," he said. "You see, it's a tree, and it has two squirrels in it. The big one is you, and the small one is me, but I didn't get to finish the eyes. I can still work on it." His mom said nothing, just looked at it. She sat down next to him, still in her uniform. "I know you worked so I could have my game, and I just wanted to give you something better than a crappy candle."

His mom held the ornament for a moment longer and then let go, and then started crying, first a little, and then a lot, putting her hands to her face. Joe paused, and then hugged her, and she hugged him back, crying into his shoulder.

"I'm sorry," said Joe. "I can make the eyes better."

"No, honey," she said. She paused, taking a big breath. She spoke through her tears. "You did great. I love you."

"I love you, too."

13

The moving shelf, filled with products, shifted in place in front of him, rotating to face the proper direction, and Joe shuffled through the items in the right bin—

Goddamnit, where was it, damn blue earbuds, no, these are white earbuds, what the hell—

Then he found them, hidden in the back of the bin, underneath a couple of kitchen towel packages, and picked them, placing them in the plastic container on the conveyor belt in front of him, and slapped the button to say the order was complete.

He took a deep breath, trying to focus. It felt like his brain was buzzing inside his head, his heart rattling inside his chest. He had gone into R&D late last night, and hadn't gotten home until nearly 4 AM, and had slept for maybe an hour before his alarm went off for his double shift the next day. Mandatory overtime. They were behind on orders again, and it was all hands on deck.

Joe had guzzled two energy drinks, and they had forestalled his exhaustion, for now, at least. But he knew he'd have to pay the piper at some point. He would buy more at lunch, force his mind to focus for the day.

But every moment he looked at the next order, he only saw Wally's undying face, all the blood drained out of it, the skin sallow. He only thought of his hands errantly moving through the air, as Nile had trained him to do, had engineered him to do. Wally's genial face, who had so kindly welcomed Joe, who had taken him out for a beer, and listened.

But more than that, more than the fact Wally had been a nice guy, but that Wally had been a loyal worker for the company. Had worked there for years, had centered his life around the job, and had trusted them. Had gone in for the promotion with the thought of improving his situation, and it had cost him everything.

Did anyone at Nile care? Did anyone even attempt to shoulder that burden of guilt?

No. They didn't.

And as Joe worked, as he picked order after order, doing his best to focus on grabbing the earbuds, the bestselling children's book, the floor mat, the spatula, and putting them in the bin, and pushing the button, all he could think about was Wally, and everyone else in those cells, and a massive rage would build inside him. A screaming anger that would overtake him, and force him, compel him to run to R&D, and destroy it all. To beat at the walls, to pummel the guards, to destroy the entire place with his bare fists.

But it would do nothing. His impotent rage would stop nothing, not right now, not if he charged the gate like a lone soldier. He'd be shot down for his trouble, beaten, arrested, lose his job, and maybe his life, if he was unlucky.

Joe hadn't talked to Anna yet, and she needed to know what was happening. She was on the inside, and she would have a better sense of what they could do. They could plan together, to do *something*, but he had to endure this double shift first, and he couldn't, his brain was going to rattle itself apart, god—

"Amery," said a voice, suddenly, and Joe jumped. He turned. It was his boss, Mr. Johnson. Johnson's face was flush. "You're behind quota today."

"I'm sorry, I'm trying my best, I had—"

"I don't care about your excuses," said Johnson. "We're behind. I need more orders picked. Find a way." And then he walked away, and Joe's anger spiked inside him, and he should just quit this damn job. Nile was monstrous, and he was right, right all along, he should have never taken the job in the first place. He should have found something else, picked a different master, one less evil, if even by a few degrees.

He couldn't keep working for them, he couldn't. There was no way he could do this much longer, not while the image of Wally lurked in his head, of the man who was sacrificed at the foot of capitalism for nothing, and left Betsy alone behind as the only one who would mourn him.

But then he remembered the guards from the night before. They knew. They knew what was happening, and they still reported for work every night.

They knew what they were signing up for.

The guards thought the dead had known the game, had known the chances. Joe very much doubted that, but did the guards really believe it? Did the doctors who injected Wally, did they know what they were doing?

Yes, of course they did. And they don't see a problem.

At least not enough of one to stop it. The money was good enough. For the guards, for the scientists, for the suits who okayed the experiments from some executive suite far away, in some city Joe would never visit, in a building Joe would never see.

Someone did the math, somewhere, about how much money they could save by using the dead to unload their shipments, to pick their orders, to ship their packages. And the number was high enough that they pushed past the legal and ethical quandaries. It didn't matter, the cost of blood or sin, the return on investment was too high. Blood for the blood god, blood for capitalism.

What if someone came sniffing? What if someone found out the truth?

Well, they wouldn't find out the truth, not until Nile had sanded it down, and removed all the hard edges. People would be upset, how could they not, but they were upset about everything else too. People hated mass shootings, they hated police violence, they hated the awful extralegal abuses the government handed out daily, but none of those things stopped, because not enough people cared enough, not enough to grab an executive and put his head under the guillotine.

Joe felt the anger rising again, and no, he needed to focus, he was behind on orders, and he didn't want to get reprimanded again by Mr. Johnson. He wanted to be finished with his day so he could talk to Anna, and they could figure out a plan. He was overwhelmed, helpless, and just one other person talking with him about it would help—

"Amery," said a voice again, and it was Johnson.

"I'm trying, I'm trying," said Joe. *Please, just leave me alone.*

"No, it's not that," said Johnson. "Boggins wants to talk to you again. They said he needed an answer from you."

"Tell them no," said Joe.

"They want to talk to you," said Johnson. "I can't answer for you."

Cold spiked his guts, and Joe stopped his work. He didn't want to talk to Boggins. Didn't want to tell him no, didn't want to say anything. Partially because he was afraid of giving away what he knew. Partially because he was afraid he would throttle Boggins in the interview room, choke him out until someone rushed into the room to pull him from Boggins' bloated corpse.

Joe clocked out and followed Johnson back to the office area of the fulfillment center, back where he had interviewed for the promotion, only a week ago. It felt like an eternity.

Boggins waited for him in the same room. Seeing him, right in front of him, he remembered again what Boggins looked like. But until this moment, Joe wouldn't be sure if he could have described his appearance. Boggins face existed to be forgotten.

"So, Mr. Amery, you've taken the entire week to think about it," said Boggins. "What's your response? We typically get answers much faster—"

"My answer is no," he said, maintaining a straight face.

He bit on the inner parts of his cheeks, to keep himself grounded.

"No?" asked Boggins. "Are you sure?"

"Yeah, I'm sure," said Joe.

"You don't want to reconsider?" asked Boggins. "The position won't be offered again—"

"No," said Joe. *Keep your answers short and to the point. You don't need to elaborate. You don't owe them an explanation.*

"Could you tell me why you're not taking the offer?" asked Boggins, staring at him, into his eyes. Joe had to look away. It felt like Boggins wasn't looking into his eyes, but through them, deeper into him. "If it's a matter of compensation, we could negotiate, and offer more, perhaps."

Jesus, even more money. But then again, they wouldn't be paying for long. They could offer him a million, but he'd never see the paycheck.

"I like my current position," said Joe. Boggins wouldn't stop staring at him, and that easy rage rose in Joe's chest. *This fucker knows what he's doing. He wants you in the lab, so they can pump you full of that shit, so you'll die, and then you'll work for them if you like it or not, until your body falls apart at the picking station, and then they'll mop you up and replace you with another fucking zombie, an endless supply of workers, fresh from the morgue—*

"That's very strange," said Boggins. "You're the first person to turn us down. I was expecting a request for higher pay, but not an outright denial." He paused, and finally looked down at his notes, and Joe felt like he could breathe again. But then Boggins' eyes cast right back up at him. "Have you spoken to anyone who was working in R&D?"

"Why does that matter?"

"We have very strict NDA agreements in place, and Nile is very serious about anyone who leaks information—"

"No," said Joe. "I haven't talked to anyone. I've been working double shifts for the past week. I've barely had time to eat and sleep. I don't want your job. I know what I have with my current position, and that's fine enough for me."

Boggins stared at him for a long second, his eyes bulging as he peered deep into Joe.

Please, let me out of here, I can't take it—

"Well, I'm sorry to hear that," said Boggins. "Good luck."

Joe mustered as much of a smile as he could and he walked out the door, trying to maintain an even pace, even as wanted to sprint away from Boggins and his eyes, and the knowledge that Boggins was doing his damned best to kill Joe and Joe just had to sit there and take it.

Joe hurried back to his workstation once he was out of sight of the offices, happy to get back to mindless work for now. He still had ten hours, still had lunch, still had so much items to pick, to do, over and over and over again.

He pushed it all away. Every thought, every feeling, he bundled them up into a ball, and swallowed it down, pushed it deep down inside him. He couldn't handle it, not right now, not if he wanted to keep working today.

So he did, and he thought of nothing, for hours on end, only the next task in his mind, drinking caffeine whenever he felt his energy lag.

And then his shifts were done, and he walked to his car, and once inside, everything boiled up at once, and Joe couldn't stop himself from crying.

The tears came hard, and Joe sobbed into his hands. He

grabbed the bundle of tissues from the console and wiped his face but it didn't hold back the tears, the emotions bubbling up and over.

He couldn't keep doing this.

He needed to talk to Anna.

14

Joe sat on Anna's couch in her small living room. She lived in an apartment on the west side of town.

Anna stood, staring at him.

"Well?" she asked. "Did you get in? Did you find anything?"

Joe nodded.

Joe had been debating about how to talk to her. About how to tell her this horrific thing. He was never good at breaking bad news.

"They killed them all, Anna," said Joe, finally, looking up at her.

"Oh, god," she said, and sat down, her legs unable to take it. Her hands went to her face. She didn't cry, though. Probably because she already had thought they were dead.

"It's worse, though," he said. She looked up.

"How could it be worse?" asked Anna. "What could be worse than killing them?"

"They're killing them," said Joe. "And then they bring them back."

"Wait—they're alive?" asked Anna. Joe saw hope in her eyes. "We can rescue them, we can save them—"

"No, Anna," said Joe. "They brought them back—as something else. There's no other way to put it—as zombies."

"What?" asked Anna. "That's impossible. This isn't the movies. You can't just bring people back."

"They had them in cages," said Joe. "I sneaked through the facility after I faked my way in. I found where they kept them. Where they kept all of them. There must have been at least thirty in there, or more. It was dark, and they were tightly packed, but there were a lot of them. And they were dead, but still standing. Still moving. But they weren't breathing."

"Maybe—maybe the drugs they give them just make it seem like they're dead. Induces a zombie-like state. That's possible—"

"They were rotting, Anna," said Joe, his voice rising. "I know what I saw. They were all in there—I saw—I saw Wally. He didn't know me. He charged the gate of the cell when he saw me."

"They're zombies?"

"Yes," said Joe. "I know it's hard to believe. But if you saw what I saw—you wouldn't doubt me." Anna stared into his eyes and then looked back down at the floor.

"But why?" asked Anna. "Why would they do that? Kill perfectly good employees? Turn them into some sort of undead creature?"

"Think about it," said Joe. "You worked with them before they died. What did you do?"

"I established a baseline," said Anna. "Tested their efficiency at different tasks. Saw how their work changed or didn't change as they took the drugs."

Joe stared at her. "None of that's true."

"Yes, it is," said Anna. "That's what I was hired for. They wanted me to improve their efficiency, to make people better workers—"

"I believe you, Anna, I do," said Joe. "And that's what they told you. What they led you to believe. But it's not your real job. Your real job is to prepare them. To prepare them for after they die. After they come back."

"What the hell does that mean?"

"I found more than just the zombies," said Joe. "I found workstations. Workstations in cages."

"Wait—no—"

"All of them, all the zombies, weren't just standing still when I found them," said Joe. "They were all moving their arms, back and forth, back and forth. Staring off into space. Moving their arms, the same way, over and over."

Anna looked at him. "They were working."

"Yeah," said Joe. "Even after death, away from their workstations, they were repeating the motions."

Anna got up, and went into the kitchen, and returned with a bottle of scotch and two small glasses.

"Do you want some?" asked Anna.

"I don't think so," said Joe. "I'm so tired. If I drank, I'd pass out."

"Fair enough," said Anna, and filled each of the glasses.

She downed one immediately and then started sipping on the other.

"You alright?" asked Joe.

"I will be," said Anna. "Not right now, though." She stared off, into space, and Joe let her have her silence for the time being. She eventually spoke again. "I was training their brains, wasn't I? As the chemical, whatever the hell it was, started working on them. I was teaching them how to do their work, even after death."

"That's what it looks like," said Joe. "I have no idea how it works. I didn't have enough time to dig through any computers. But there were a lot of chemicals."

"The perfect employee," said Anna. "Never eats, never sleeps, never stops. But—but how do they keep the bodies stable, if they're dead?"

"I don't think they do," said Joe. "I heard the guards talking. I think they intend to work them until they rot away. And then replace them."

"It's monstrous," said Anna. "It's inhuman. It's illegal. They can't get away with it. There's no way they will. We have to do something."

"That's why I'm here," said Joe. "I want to do something. I wanted to talk to you first. You're on the inside. You know more about how they operate."

"Yeah, more," said Anna. "But still not much. They keep us all siloed off from each other. Everyone knows only as much as they need to."

"We have to do *something*," said Joe.

"I mean, we do," said Anna. "We'll go to the police."

"What will they do?"

"They'll arrest people," said Anna. "They'll stop it—"

"Why would they do that?" asked Joe. "What evidence do we have?"

"We both work there," said Anna. "You've seen it, first hand—"

"I saw it while I was trespassing," said Joe. "And I didn't take any pictures, even if that would make a difference. They won't take my word for it."

"There are people missing!" said Anna. "There's evidence of that!"

"They purposefully chose employees who have no family, little friends. No one who would miss them. They isolated them on purpose. They hid their vehicles after the fact. And yes, eventually, maybe, if we contacted the police and told them about the missing people, they'd do something. They'd start an investigation. But could they get a warrant into Nile's lab with that?"

"I don't know," said Anna. "But what else can we do? Go to the news, maybe."

"Again, it would take a long time," said Joe. "Weeks or months. And sure, they might get the evidence we need. But in the meantime, more people dying. More people suffering. More zombies."

"Then what the hell are we supposed to do?"

"You can get us in, right?"

"Into the lab?" asked Anna. "Yeah, I guess. I could probably come up with a reason for us to go in together—"

"Then that's what we do."

"And do what?"

"We destroy everything," said Joe. "All of their research. All of their chemicals. We make them start over."

"We can't do that, Joe," said Anna. "The guards will stop

us."

"Not if we work fast," said Joe. "There are no cameras in there. The guards on duty barely cared about anything. They won't check on you. They'll think you're doing your job."

"I—" Anna swallowed another sip of her scotch.

"What is it?" asked Joe. "We can gather evidence as we go, and give it to the news after. Find someone we can trust, a big reporter, and they'll break the story. Hit them hard."

Anna took a deep breath and exhaled. "It's my career, Joe. They'll know it was me. No one will hire me after this."

"What are you talking about?" asked Joe. "Why wouldn't they hire you? You'll have done nothing wrong."

"I'll have broken into the company I worked for and committed sabotage, Joe," said Anna.

"They're killing people!"

"Yeah, they're killing people," said Anna, her voice calm now. "But the other companies don't care. They'd only see that I won't follow the rules. That I won't honor confidentiality agreements—"

"That you'll do the right thing."

"That's part of the problem," said Anna. "You know that. You're not naive. Every big company breaks rules. Some of them are innocuous. Some are a little sketchy. And sometimes it costs people's lives. But no one wants to hire a whistle blower. Because that's what I'll be for the rest of my life. No matter where I go. I'll be blacklisted forever."

She took another sip of scotch.

"Anna, I need you to get inside," said Joe. "I can't pull the delivery trick again. Hell, I'll probably have to wear a disguise to get in with you. This doesn't work without you."

She stared into his eyes, and then looked away. "We

could just forget it."

"What? You can't be serious," said Joe. "People are dead. People are zombies!"

"Nile killed people last year, Joe," said Anna. "43 people died when a tornado hit the warehouse they were working in. People wanted permission to leave because of storm conditions. Manager said no. Said they were behind on orders."

"That's different—"

"Is it?" asked Anna. "I knew about that before I was hired, Joe. And if you didn't, I can't believe you aren't aware of all the other terrible things they've done. The many, many small businesses they've strong armed. The way they've reshaped our economy, avoided paying taxes, and obviously, all the ways they abuse and use workers without regard to their humanity."

"Of course I knew."

"How is this different?" asked Anna. "Why is this abuse worse than the others? Because it's zombies? Yeah, it's insane, obviously, but it's no worse than them running some middle-aged woman into the ground, working her so hard she died from cancer. That happened, too. Last year."

"It's different because I saw it, Anna," said Joe. "Because I swallowed all those things down because I needed a job. I needed to pay for my mom's care, and I needed to get my own apartment, so I got in bed with the devil, and they're all devils. But I was nervous on my first day, and Wally came up to me and said hello. He bought me a beer that night, and we talked about how work sucks. I met Betsy. And I heard him talk. Heard him talk about how this new position would change his life. He said he was going to get Betsy a new doghouse." Joe wiped away a tear. "And now he's dead.

And they don't give a single shit about him. He's nothing but grist for the mill. And maybe it's a stupid thing to do, to not just go to the police or some journalist, and hope it works out. But I'm tired of sitting on the sidelines and doing nothing. Sure, it might cost me, cost you. But I don't care. I'm so goddamn angry, and I want them to pay, in some small way, for once."

Anna swallowed the last of her second glass of scotch.

"Okay," said Anna. "When do you want to do it?"

15

Anna told him she would start looking into things at work. Figure out a plan for them to get in, and do something. Told him it would take some time, and she would let him know when she was ready. Until then, he should lie low. Go to work. Operate as normally.

He did his best. Wally's rotting face still lingered when he closed his eyes.

*

Joe's mom smiled wide when she saw him come into her room. She was sitting in her recliner, the television on the home and garden channel. They were flipping old houses.

"I'm so glad to see you," she said, her arms out. She

pushed herself out of the chair with a grunt and met him a few steps away from it.

"You don't have to get up," said Joe.

"Oh please," she said. "I'm not immobile yet. And I haven't seen you in weeks."

"I've been real busy."

"Please, please, honey, you can have the seat. I'll sit on my helper chair."

"Mom—" he started, but she had already unfolded her walker into a seat and sat down. He sunk into her recliner.

"How are you doing, sweetheart?" she asked, staring at him.

Well, my work is trying to turn me into a zombie—

"I'm alright," said Joe. "Tired."

"I was going to ask, are you getting enough sleep? You seem to be dragging a little bit."

"As much as I can," said Joe. It didn't help that every time he closed his eyes he saw the face of Wally staring at him, his eyes vacant and filled with blood.

"Is it your new job?" asked his mom. "Are they working you too hard?"

"It's a lot of work," said Joe. "A lot of double shifts and mandatory overtime."

"I always liked getting overtime. It meant a little extra money for grocery shopping that week."

"But you didn't do it every day," said Joe. "And you never *had* to do it, did you?"

His mom stopped to think. "No, I don't think so," she said. "I was desperate, Joe. I had to support you, and with your dad not around, I didn't have much of a choice."

"I know," said Joe. "I know. I worked 70 hours last week."

"Jeez, Joe," said his mom. "That is a lot."

"Yeah," said Joe. "It's wearing on me." *In more ways than one.*

"Like I said, I don't have to be in here—"

"No, Mom," said Joe. "I'm not complaining. You did so much for me, for so long. It's time to return the favor."

She whispered something, not quite under her breath.

"What'd you say, Mom?"

"It's not supposed to work like that."

"Work like what?"

"That I spend my life raising you, and supporting you, and working myself to the bone for you, and then you have to turn around and do the same for me after my body gives up the ghost. I'm supposed to retire with a nest egg, and maybe even leave you something when I'm gone for good—"

"Don't say that, Mom," said Joe.

"No, no," she said. "It's only a matter of time, Joe. And trying to ignore it won't make it disappear. I've had a lot of time to think in here, and I know you don't want to hear it, but I won't be around forever. I'm not quite at the end of the road, but I'm getting there. I can see it from here, and lying to myself about it won't do either you or me any good. I'm just sorry—sorry that I'm not leaving you anything. No house, no inheritance. No stocks. No future."

She looked away from him, toward the window, which overlooked the back of the property, with some grass and a few trees bordered by a wooden fence.

"You don't have to apologize to me, Mom," said Joe. "You did your best. You did what you could."

"It's our fault."

"Who's fault?" asked Joe. "What are you talking about?"

"It's hard for me to understand," she said. "I try, I really do. But things have changed so much. I worked as a waitress and I was able to raise you on that. Nowadays, that's not enough, is it?"

Joe looked at her. "It might be, if you got good tips and consistent hours. But most servers work a couple of jobs, at least, and probably drive for Uber in their spare time."

"It's just business," she said. "That's what they said, you know, when they fired me from the restaurant. It's just business. I couldn't work anymore, and I was losing them money. So they fired me."

"It wasn't right."

"I know," said his mom. "But there was a part of me that understood. And that's what I mean. I should have been royally pissed. I should have been so angry, I should have screamed. I didn't, though. I said thank you, and then I hung up."

"You had gone through a lot—"

"I was thankful," she said. "But why was I thankful? I gave them my life, Joe. I worked for years, pounding my feet and ankles into those hard floors, shouldering entrees for rich folk who tipped 10 percent if I was lucky. Who would order a hundred dollar lunch and not think a moment about it. And when I *finally* clawed my way into the office, at a desk, my body gave out on me."

"It's not your fault," said Joe. "You couldn't control that. It's a miracle you survived at all."

"Just business," she said. "We made it acceptable. We just nodded, and said thank you. It's our fault things are like this. My fault."

"No, it's not," said Joe. "You're only one person. You were busy trying to survive. Raising me. You're not responsible for all of society."

"Sometimes it feels that way," she said. "And I look at you, and you're no better off than I am. Worse, even. Working seventy-hour weeks." She sighed, and looked back at Joe. "Listen to me, opining about the state of things. I'm getting soft in my old age, Joe."

"You're not old," said Joe. He had always said that over the years. When he was little, and his mom turned 40, and when he was a teen, and she turned 50, and when he was in his 20s, and she turned 60. Now she neared 70, and he still said it. Before, he wasn't lying. But as the years went on, he believed it less and less. And now, it *was* a lie.

His mother was old.

She smiled at him. "You're too sweet." Her smile faded. "Maybe you'll work it out. It looks like you might, even with all the problems in the world."

"Work what out?"

"Everything," she said. "You'll pick up the pieces. Fix what we broke."

*

"You said we shouldn't meet. You said I should keep my head down," said Joe, sitting down at the bar. Anna sat alone, a rocks glass half full in front of her.

"You came," she said, glancing at him.

"Yeah," said Joe. They sat alone, the place mostly empty on a lonely Wednesday night. They were a forty-five minute drive from Springfield. The chances of seeing anyone who knew them here was slim. The bar was a dive, and classic rock played distantly over the speakers.

Joe ordered a beer, and the bartender dropped it off and left them alone.

"I'm guessing you haven't made any progress," said Joe.

"Not anything substantial," said Anna. "I'm still poking around. Don't want to make too big a wave."

Joe took a sip of his beer. "Then why—"

"I needed to talk to someone."

Joe glanced over at her. Anna stared ahead, her eyes scanning the back of the bar.

"How are you holding up?"

"Not well, Joe," said Anna. "Not well."

"We're going to stop them," said Joe. "We will."

Anna said nothing, taking a sip of her liquor. "Her name is Sue. *Was* Sue. She loved soap operas. She recorded Days of Our Lives every day, and would talk about the stories with me in all our sessions. I never watched, but she was so invested in them. And she loved all the characters. Even the bad guys. I think she liked them the most, even if she hated them, if that makes sense. She watched all the episodes. Sue bought all the magazines. She was going to get a big home theater system, you know. Surround sound, 4K, with a really nice recliner, so she could watch her stories when she got home."

Anna stopped, reached into her purse, and pulled out a tissue, and wiped her eyes, and blew her nose. She paused, and they sat in silence for a couple of minutes. She turned and looked at Joe, finally.

"She didn't come in today," said Anna. "She's dead. One of those things, now. No more stories for Sue. And no home theater system. Nile killed her."

"You didn't—"

"I didn't stop it," said Anna. "I couldn't. Couldn't do a thing." She took another sip. "I didn't want to do this, you know. I wanted to get a history degree. I love history. I wanted to study. But I knew it wouldn't get me a career, not in anything but teaching history. So I studied something practical. I knew it would get me a job with someone, like Nile, or Apple, or any of the big companies. They all could use someone like me. And I found it interesting, I did. But I never slowed down to think about what the work was. About how all of it was about turning humans into machines. Making them more efficient. I never stopped to think about the ethics of it. About the need for it. Why do we need to be more efficient? Why do we need to scrape every dollar from someone?"

Anna exhaled.

"You're one person," said Joe. "The burden of the whole system doesn't lie on you. And when you realized something was wrong, after we talked, you changed. You didn't put your head in the sand. We're doing the right thing."

Anna swallowed the last of her liquor. "This whiskey is not good."

Joe laughed. "You still finished it."

"I don't believe in wasting whiskey. Even if it's bad."

The bartender came over, and Anna ordered a pour of something else.

"More?" asked Joe.

"You just got your beer," said Anna. "I don't have anywhere else to be."

*

It was raining when he got back to Helen's. Betsy sprinted at him, her tail wagging like crazy. He hugged her and pet her hard, and she lapped up the attention. Helen was in the kitchen, cooking.

"Has she been walked lately?" asked Joe.

"No," said Helen. "I was going to do it, but I was hoping it would stop raining. I don't think it's going to."

Joe looked down at Betsy's wide eyes, staring up at him. She whined slightly. "I'll take her. I'm already wet." Joe grabbed her leash and latched it onto her collar, and went right back outside.

"Do you like the rain, Betsy?" asked Joe. Betsy responded by walking right out into the downpour, from under the slim protection of the overhang. Joe followed her as she pulled on the leash. "Guess so."

He walked Betsy. He had already been wet, but now he was soaked, the rain drenching his hoodie, and getting to his shirt underneath. Even his socks were wet. Betsy did her business, and he walked her back to Helen's.

Helen was at the door with a towel, and she wiped off Betsy's paws.

"Thanks," she said, as they came in, and Joe wiped his feet. "I made us dinner, after you've changed."

"Oh," said Joe. "Thanks. I'll be ready in a few."

He changed out of his wet clothes. Helen had made spaghetti and meatballs, and it was waiting for him on her small dining room table. Helen sat there, too.

"You didn't have to wait for me," said Joe.

"It's okay," said Helen. Joe's stomach was growling, and he ate. It hit the spot. They ate in silence, but Helen eventually spoke up. "Are you okay?"

"I'm alright."

"You've been working a lot," she said. "And you've seemed tense, or anxious, or something, and I know I've been hard to deal with—"

"Helen, you don't have to—"

"No," she said. "I wanted to say I'm sorry. I wasn't fair to you. You were trying your best, and your mom's situation put a lot of pressure on you. And everything I did probably didn't help. I had a lot of stress from work, and I let too much of it out on you."

"You let me stay here," said Joe. "I get it. And you let me keep Betsy."

"How could I not?" asked Helen. Betsy looked up from under the table at them, her tongue sticking out. "And after losing her owner like that—"

Joe had told her Wally had gotten sick and died. Not strictly a lie. "She's a good dog." He looked at Helen. "I get my first paycheck on Friday. It should be good. I can help with the rent, if you want."

"You don't have to," said Helen. "You should try and build up some savings, so you can stand on your own two feet again."

"I'm trying," he said. "I'm trying." He thought to Anna, to Nile's secrets. To their plan to upend everything.

"You're doing great," said Helen, mustering a smile. "Betsy thinks so, too." Betsy licked his hand, as if on cue.

"I wish things were simpler."

"What do you mean?" asked Helen.

"I don't know," said Joe. He paused. "Working for Nile is difficult. And I don't mean the work. It *is* hard, but knowing I'm helping this awful company—"

"I know it's hard," said Helen. "But you didn't decide that this is the world we live in. You were born into it, like everyone else. You can only do what you need to survive."

"We only have each other," said Joe, quietly.

"What?"

"It was something Wally told me," said Joe. "I think about it a lot."

"You rescued Betsy, when you didn't have to," said Helen. "You're taking care of your mom. What else can you do?"

*

Joe kept working, keeping his head down, and doing his best to be an efficient employee, and avoid suspicion. He didn't have any more meetings with Boggins, and Mr. Johnson had no more criticism of him. He got his first paycheck in. It was good, as he had predicted. He put some in the bank. He used some to pay for his mother's care.

He used the rest to buy a pistol.

Anna called him, eventually, late at night.

"Are you ready?"

16

"Tomorrow night," said Anna.

They sat in her apartment. Anna was sipping on the same scotch. Joe wondered if that continued even after he left. It was better not to ask.

"What's the plan?" asked Joe.

"I've been keeping my eyes open," said Anna. "And I think I have something."

"Don't they watch you?"

"Oh, all the time," said Anna. "But they're understaffed. They can't keep track of everything. As long as it looks like you're keeping normal routines, and you're not asking for more pay, or going into departments you're not supposed to, they assume you're following the straight and narrow. There's a scientist in R&D. Dr. Steven Petry. He has high-level access. His key can get us anywhere in the building."

"Okay," said Joe. "That's a good start. How are we going to get it?"

"Ask me how I know this information about Petry," said Anna. She took a sip of her scotch and looked at Joe knowingly.

"How?" asked Joe. He'd bite.

"I asked him," said Anna, smiling a slight, wry smile.

"And he just told you all this sensitive information about what access he has?"

"Dr. Petry has a crush on me," said Anna. "It's very obvious, at least to me. Probably to anyone else as well. But he was quite happy to talk to me over lunch."

"And that conversation turned casually into what access he has."

"Well, yes," said Anna. "I let him brag about it, and pretended to be impressed."

"What is he in charge of?" asked Joe. "Is he one of the researchers?"

"He's the head of Applications."

"What the hell is that?"

"His team comes up with ways to sell the technologies and research Nile does, among probably other things. I don't know, I didn't delve too deeply, because I didn't want to make him suspicious."

"But he has high-level access?"

"Yes," said Anna. "Anything we would need to get to, he can get us in."

"How do we get to him?"

"Oh, that's easy," said Anna. "I asked him to meet after hours, tomorrow night. I said I needed help with some practical applications for my work. Said I wanted to get ahead, but I didn't have any time during the day. Asked if he'd meet me later."

"And he said yes," said Joe. "Maybe hoping you're asking for more than just help with your work."

"Oh, he's absolutely hoping," said Anna. "He's going to get more than he bargained for. Only question is how we're going to coerce him—"

"I have the answer for that," said Joe. He reached into the back of the waistband of his jeans and pulled out the pistol.

"Jesus, Joe," said Anna. He put it on the table in front of them. "Do you know how to work that thing?"

"It's not complicated," said Joe. "I've taken it to the range a couple times, but ultimately, you point it at the thing you want to destroy, and pull the trigger. I think it'll do the job."

Anna took a deep breath. "Fair enough."

"If we're going to do this, we need to do it right. That means more than just destroying the facility, or the chemicals—we have to destroy all their research. Everything on the computers, on their servers, on anything, anywhere."

"Petry can get us in there," said Anna. "And with the proper motivation, he'll delete it all." She eyed the gun.

"Except for one copy."

"One?"

"Yes," said Joe. "Like you said. We save a copy, and give it to a journalist, along with photos of what we find inside. The facility will be worthless, and then Nile will have the spotlight on them. What time tomorrow?"

"I told him ten."

"How are you going to get me in?"

"That'll be the tricky part."

"I think it'll all be the tricky part."

"Well, security won't want to let you in," said Anna. "We don't allow guests, ever, unless they're rich folk invited in by execs. So, we'll have to lie."

"What's our story?"

"You're one of the test subjects," said Anna. "And I'm bringing you in to do more tests. Have to get them done before the next day."

"But you're not in charge of that."

"No, I'm not," said Anna. "But do they know that?" She took a sip of scotch.

"Well, do they?"

"I don't know," said Anna. "If they don't, we can bluff our way in. If they do, we may bluff our way in, regardless. Or, they might stop us before we begin."

"It's a risk we have to take," said Joe. "It seems like they don't know much. They weren't surprised by the zombies, though. I don't know how word hasn't gotten out."

"Fear."

"Yeah, I'm sure," said Joe. "But if it was anonymously leaked, Nile couldn't punish *everyone*. They wouldn't be able to know who it was that leaked—"

"The list is shorter than you think," said Anna. "I worked there, and I didn't know. Not really. I suspected, but that's a different thing altogether, and I had no evidence of any wrongdoing. Anybody who could know, who does know, well, they're afraid. And Nile *could* punish everyone, quite easily."

"They wouldn't fire them," said Joe. "Not anyone in a prominent position. They couldn't afford to lose them."

"It wouldn't be anyone in a high position," said Anna.

"They're paid too much. They understand the game at this point. The guards would be most likely, but they get paid a lot as well, especially for just sitting at a desk and doing nothing. No one is going to leak anything. And anyone Nile suspected of leaking—well, they'd disappear."

"They can't just make anyone disappear."

"All those workers, all those test subjects," said Anna. "What happened to them?"

"Yeah, but they were targeted," said Joe. "Nile recruited specifically because they had little personal connections outside of work."

"And I moved here alone, Joe," said Anna. "I don't really have any friends. My family lives thousands of miles away. They wouldn't know I was missing until days had passed. Maybe weeks. We don't talk very much."

"Why not?" asked Joe. "I mean, you don't have to tell me—"

"It's nothing bad," said Anna. "We're just busy. It gets hard, and it gets pushed aside. I should call my parents tomorrow at lunch. Just to say hi."

"To remind them you're alive," said Joe.

"Yeah, something like that," said Anna. "But people go missing all the time. And Nile has the resources to make it look like a dozen other things." She paused. "I'm just saying all this because before we go in, we need to understand. If things go wrong, in one of a thousand ways—we might not come out."

Anna took a sip of scotch. Her glass was almost empty. "You don't have to come with me. I can do this alone."

"Anna, we—"

"You have nothing to do with this," said Anna. "You're

just trying to pay your bills, working at the fulfillment center. You didn't help them. *I* helped them. I looked those people in the eyes as they did their tasks, as whatever fucking poison they put in them rotted them from the inside out. I watched them slowly die, and then disappear from my lab, and I dismissed it. *I* let it happen. If it wasn't for you—" Anna paused, and wiped away a tear. "If it wasn't for you, I'd probably still be doing it. So, thank you. Thank you for waking me up. But you don't have to stay in this. You can leave it to me. You don't need to pay for this."

Anna downed the rest of her scotch and wiped her lips.

Joe took a deep breath, and exhaled, and looked at Anna. "You can't do this alone, Anna. You need backup."

"Not necessarily. I can handle Petry on my own, and without you, the guards won't be suspicious—"

"You need help," said Joe. "And there's no one else."

"That's not a good enough reason—"

"I want to help, Anna," said Joe. "I've always said that I want to help. But what have I done? What have I done that's actually helpful? Posted about corrupt companies on social media. Annoyed my friends, when they order something from Nile, or shop at Walmart. *Sometimes* not use those companies, until I really have to, or because I can't afford not to. But no matter what I do, my entire life, nothing has changed. My choices have affected nothing. Nile has grown and grown and grown. All the big companies have. It doesn't matter who I vote for, or how strongly I feel—it doesn't matter. They're too big, too powerful, and I can't change anything. And I don't know about you, but I'm fucking sick of it. I get so angry—I can feel it down in my bones. It's just impotent fucking rage, and it's been there my entire adult life. As I've been fucked over, repeatedly, and nothing I do *matters*." Joe took another breath. "Well, here's my chance. I can hurt them. I can do something about them, something real. Make them lose something. And yes, I'm terrified. I was terrified the other night, too. But there was something else. And I thought about it, and I realized what it was. It was purpose. I had a purpose. And after what they did to Wally. What they did to all those people. What they were going to do to *me*—I'm so fucking angry, there's no way in hell I'm not going in there with you."

"I only have one question then," said Anna. "What do we do with the zombies?"

Joe stared at her. "I assumed, you know, that we'd kill them. Again. There's nothing in there anymore."

"They're our strongest piece of evidence against Nile," said Anna. "They're direct proof of what Nile has done, and what happened to all those people. It's not theoretical. It's real, and has been tested on people."

"It's not like we can wrangle them, and walk them to the authorities," said Joe. "They seem like wild animals, honestly, and I don't know what they'd do if we let them out."

"I don't know if I can," said Anna. "I know, you told me what you saw, but still, it's hard for me to process killing someone, even in the state they're in."

"Don't worry, I'll handle it. When we get there, I'll cross that bridge."

"You sure?"

"Yeah," said Joe. "It'll be a mercy."

17

Joe squeezed the pistol in his hand. His hands were in the front pocket of his hoodie, the gun clutched in one of them. His sweat made the grip slippery, and he tried to wipe it, and he felt for the safety, yes it was on, he didn't want to shoot himself, jesus christ—

"You ready?" asked Anna. They sat in her car in the parking lot.

"I guess," said Joe. He squeezed the pistol again. He saw Wally's face.

Wally, alive in his living room, petting Betsy.

Wally, dead, staring off into space, in a cell deep in Nile's labs.

"Let's go," said Anna, and they got out, hurrying to the entrance to R&D. Joe pulled his hoodie up. They had used makeup to mark dark circles under his eyes, to color his face. He looked sickly, unwell. It had been Anna's idea, and he hoped it would help. The guards would look at him, and see he was sick, dying, and not think too deeply about why she was bringing him in at 10 o'clock at night.

He followed her, the gun weighing heavy in his front pocket. He cradled it between his hands. If the guards stopped them—should he pull the pistol? He hadn't asked Anna beforehand, and now they were at the door, and through, and it was too late. He squeezed the cold metal, slick with sweat.

Joe stayed behind Anna, trying to stay out of view of the two guards, who looked up from their phones, and they both stood now, seeing two people come in, one of them being Anna. This was unusual, and Joe's eyes went to the second guard's hand, which lingered near his waist, near his holster. Joe averted his eyes, looking away from them, keeping part of his face obscured. He had let his stubble grow out, and combed what little hair he could over his forehead. Would they even remember the delivery guy from a week ago, who had only appeared once?

No, of course not, they saw hundreds of people—

But the whisper in the back of Joe's mind told him they knew him, and knew they were lying, and this would be the end, before it even began.

"Dr. Marshall?" asked the first guard. "Strange to see you here so late. Who's this?"

"Hi, Gary," said Anna. "I needed to come in unexpectedly. We need some findings before tomorrow. This is one of the test subjects, John. We'll be going to my lab and doing some work there."

Gary looked at her, his eyes confused. "John?" asked Gary. His eyes went to Joe, but Joe didn't look at him. He only looked down and did his best to look tired and sick. "Is he new?"

"He started a few days ago," said Anna. "Well, we'll be in my lab if you need anything," said Anna, and walked forward.

"Wait a second," said Gary.

Damn it.

"I'm sorry, Dr. Marshall, but we can't let more than one person in at a time after hours," said Gary. "Especially a lab ra—a test subject."

"Well, I need the results," said Anna. "I can't get them without a subject. I'm up against a deadline, guys, one which I wasn't expecting, and do I want to have to work at night, when I should be home, sleeping? No, of course not, but I don't have a choice. And I woke up John here, and got him to come overnight with double pay, and now we'll have to pay him even more—"

"It's against policy, Doctor," said Gary. "They'll rip me apart if I let you both in—"

Joe felt the gun in his hands. The second guard was still staring at him. He felt his eyes on him, on his hoodie. It wasn't brisk enough outside to warrant it, but maybe the guard realized that Joe was sick and needed the extra warmth. Or maybe he thought Joe had a pistol in his hands, and that's why the guard kept his hand close to his holster.

They needed to get inside. Some bullshit about policy or routine—

"Fine," said Anna. She pulled out her phone, and poked at it with her finger. "I didn't want to—"

"What are you doing?"

"I'm calling Mr. Boggins," she said, holding the phone up to her ear.

"Wait, wait, wait—"

"Who do you think I owe the results to?" asked Anna. "So, if you need approval to let me in to my own lab, well, he's the one who can do it. I'm sure he'll appreciate you two keeping me from working. As well as waking him up."

"Okay, okay," said Gary. "Please, hang up."

Anna stared at him for a long second and then touched her phone again.

"You don't have to bring Boggins into this," said Gary.

"Can I please get into my lab, then?" asked Anna. "Just don't log John in. It'll be fine. We'll only be in there a few hours, and then we'll be gone. No one will know the difference."

Joe watched Gary, his eyes glancing over at him, darting away before being seen. He was there to work. He had been woken up in the middle of the night, he wouldn't be angry, only annoyed. The cold steel of the pistol felt stark in his hands.

It felt like forever, there, and Joe's guts ached. His heart thumped in his chest, like it would rattle his ribcage apart, it was beating so hard, and they saw he was nervous, he was ready to pull the gun—

"Fine," said Gary. "You can take him in."

"Thank you," said Anna, giving a small smile, and then she moved, using her access card to get them into the lab, past the guards.

They were through the door, and Joe could breathe again. He realized he'd been holding his breath.

"Jesus," said Joe.

"It's fine," said Anna. "We're in. Step one finished."

"Only a dozen more to go."

"We're doing well," said Anna. "Next, we find Petry, and we convince him to help us."

"Where are we meeting him?"

"I told him to wait for me in my lab," said Anna. "We're running a couple minutes late."

"Does he know I'm with you?"

"No," said Anna. "You'll be a surprise. Wait outside the door for a minute, and I'll distract him, and then you come in."

"Will he be armed?"

"I highly doubt it," said Anna. "He's a pencil pusher. He's very smart, but I don't think he's expecting any of this."

"He only has eyes for you."

"Yes," said Anna. "I'm sure it'll be a shock." She looked at him as they walked. They had gone a different way than before, Anna moving confidently. She stopped, and waved her keycard, and they went through a door, and there was another hallway, and another door, and another hallway.

"How far is your lab?"

"Not far," said Anna. "Two more hallways. Can you do this?"

"What?"

"You look nervous."

"I *am* nervous. But that doesn't mean I can't do it," said Joe. "You said he knows, right?"

"Yes," said Anna. "With the amount of access he has, and how high up he is in the company, he knows. Probably more than most."

Joe squeezed the pistol in his hand. "Then it won't be a problem."

Anna held his gaze for a second, and then looked forward. They stopped at a door. "It's past this door, through another hallway, and then we'll be there. I assume he'll be in my office, but I can't be sure. Be ready."

Joe nodded and then they went through, into another hallway, this one short with only a couple of doors. Anna went to the farthest door on the left. She waited outside. She leaned into his ear and whispered.

"This is it. I'm assuming he's inside. Give me one minute, and then come in, as quiet as you can. I'll have his back to the door. With any luck, he won't see or hear you coming. Don't let the door close fully, or it'll lock. Got it?"

Joe nodded, meeting her eyes. Anna took a deep breath and then waved her key card, and pulled the door open, going inside. Joe grabbed a hold of the handle and slowly let it shut, holding right before the deadbolt clicked through. He tested it, moving it just slightly. It was open. He could hear them inside.

"I'm sorry I'm late," said Anna.

"Oh, it's only a few minutes," said Petry. His voice sounded like a professor Joe had in college before he dropped out. Thin and reedy, but quiet. "How are you?"

"I'm good," said Anna. "Thank you again for taking the time. I know it's late, but I didn't want any distractions."

Anna had said a minute, and Joe took her literally. He started counting as soon as she went in.

50, 49, 48

"It's no problem at all," said Petry. "I like to be as helpful as possible to newer employees. It helps create a better workplace."

"I wanted to talk about that," said Anna.

37, 36, 35

"Anything," said Petry. Joe pulled the pistol out of his hoodie with his right hand, holding it free now, hanging by his side, the door handle still clutched in his left. He squeezed both, as Anna sweet-talked Petry.

"Will you help me at my station to start?" asked Anna. "I want to look at my results and see if you can pick out what's wrong with them. I've been poring over them for days, and I just can't seem to find the error."

22, 21, 20

"Let me take a good look," said Petry. And then silence.

8, 7, 6

"Here's the overview, if that helps," said Anna.

3, 2, 1

Joe took a deep breath and squeezed the gun. He pulled open the door slowly. It was silent, the hinges well-oiled. He peeked inside, worried Petry would be staring right at him, but Anna had done her job well. Petry was sitting at Anna's workstation, his back to the door, a big monitor in front of him. He was staring at the screen, his eyes close to it. Anna stood to one side, and glanced at Joe, seeing him, and then put her arm around Petry, ensuring he wouldn't turn around.

"See anything?" asked Anna.

Joe held the pistol up, pointed at Petry. He squeezed it hard and turned off the safety. He moved up behind him, stepping quietly, the pistol never veering from the back of Petry's head. Joe was right behind him now.

"Anna, I don't see anything amiss. There might be nothing wrong at all—"

Joe put the gun to the back of Petry's head, pressing hard.

"I think if we look a little harder, Doctor, we might find something."

18

"What is this—"

Joe pressed the barrel hard into Petry's head.

"You do the wrong thing or say the wrong words and the contents of your head will be replaced by the contents of this gun, understand?"

"Yes, yes, I understand," said Petry. "Who are you, what is going on, Anna—"

Petry looked at her and saw her lack of surprise.

"Oh, this is your doing," said Petry. Anna stared back, stonefaced.

"Not entirely," she said. "But partially."

"I don't know what you want, but I can't give it to you," said Petry.

"I don't think that's true, Doctor," said Joe. "I think

you can do exactly what we need. Anna tells me you have high-level access to Nile's systems. That you can get us into the computer, and into any lab we want."

"You won't be able to steal from Nile," said Petry. "They trace everything. The moment it gets to a competitor, they'll know where it came from, and shut it down. They have the best lawyers in the world—"

"Why do you think we're trying to steal something?"

"Why the hell else would you be here?" asked Petry. Joe spun the office chair around, Petry now facing Joe. His head was covered in thinning blonde hair, with thick-framed glasses on his face. He looked like every middle manager Joe had ever had.

Joe held the pistol between Petry's eyes.

"Look at me, Doctor," said Joe. "I want to see your eyes."

Petry stared at him, a mixture of confusion, anger, and fear. Joe stared back.

"Do you know, Doctor?" asked Joe. "Anna's pretty sure you do, but I want to be sure."

"Know what?" asked Petry.

Joe eyed him. "Them. Doctor. The dead. The ones that you killed, and then brought back."

Petry's face remained still. A lip twitch here, a nostril flare there. He tried to keep a poker face. But his eyes widened, just for a moment. Not in surprise. But in fear, knowing that Joe knew.

"What is that supposed to mean?"

Joe stared at him and sneered. He knew. Not a doubt in Joe's mind.

It was a small blessing. It would make this easier.

"Cute," said Joe. "But I've had bosses lie to me a lot in my life. You'll have to do better than that. Let's go." Joe gestured with the pistol.

"Go where?" asked Petry.

"Your workstation," said Joe. "I assume that's where you have the most access. Computer first. Lead us to your office."

Petry cautiously stood up, and then looked at Anna. "What are you doing, Anna, joining up with this criminal, whatever your plan is, you won't get away with it, you'll never work again—"

Anna slapped him, hard, across the cheek, her right hand moving fast, a gunshot sounding in the room. Petry looked shocked, holding his face.

"You shut your fucking mouth," said Anna. "You helped them do this. How dare you."

Petry stared at her for a long second, cradling his face.

"Get moving," said Joe, gesturing with the gun again. "Your office."

Petry walked, glaring at Joe, and then Joe walked behind him, the gun on his back. They left Anna's office, and then down the hallway. Joe leaned into Anna's ear.

"Stop him if he's leading us the wrong way," whispered Joe. Anna nodded, but as Petry walked she said nothing, and they followed him through another hallway, another door. It was a maze back here, and Joe was lost. He kept his eyes open for security, and kept the pistol squeezed tight in his hands, if Petry would try anything. Yell for help, or run.

But Petry did nothing, except lead them to his office. He waved his key card over the electronic lock and it buzzed open, like all the others had.

His office wasn't anything special. It was big, but plain, with a bookshelf and degrees on the wall. Some pictures of smiling people that Joe didn't recognize. His desk was large, and three screens sat upon it, along with a mess of paperwork.

"Behind the desk," said Joe. "Sit down. Log in. Do what Anna tells you to do."

"This won't impact anything," said Petry. "You can't stop—"

Joe reared back and hit him once with the butt of the pistol. Petry fell back with a grunt, slamming into the floor.

"You speak when spoken to," said Joe. "Get up. Behind the desk. Do what Anna says, or I hit you again."

Petry glared at him from the floor, from behind his thick glasses, but said nothing, pushing himself up. Petry got behind the computer. Joe stood behind him, the gun staying on him.

Joe's shoulder ached from holding the pistol aloft, but he held it still.

Anna stood next to Petry. "Go to the directory where we keep all the information on the zombie project." Petry looked up at her, doing nothing.

"Now, Doctor," said Joe. "I *will* shoot you."

Petry took a breath and turned on the computer, letting it boot up and signing in. Anna watched, and Joe kept an eye on her. Anna would know if he was doing what they said.

Joe watched as Petry typed, and clicked on different programs. He finally entered a screen with long lines of text.

"Well?" asked Petry.

Anna handed him a thumb drive. "Copy all of it onto this."

Petry grabbed the drive with derision and slid it into the

USB port on the front of his tower.

"So, you are just stealing," said Petry. "Acting all high and mighty—"

"We're taking it to the press," said Joe. "You kill people for a living, Petry. You don't have the moral high ground."

"I haven't killed anyone," said Petry. "Not a single person."

"Oh, you haven't?" asked Joe. "The room full of corpses tells a different story."

"They volunteered," said Petry. "They knew the risks."

"You don't believe that," said Joe.

"It's very clear in their paperwork that there's risk involved with the position—"

"It's funny that you think that paperwork absolves your company of fucking killing people and turning them into goddamn undead slaves," said Joe.

"I didn't inject anyone with anything," said Petry, his voice louder. "I don't even work on the project directly, I only see the reports—"

"Wally was his name," said Joe.

"What the hell are you talking about—"

"Wally Foegle," said Joe. "He worked at Nile for 3 years. He was in his 50s. He was on his feet for ten hours a day. His body was a mess of knee braces and elbow sleeves, just so he could keep up with the work. He worked hard and never complained—"

"What does this—"

"You shut your mouth and listen," said Joe. "His name was Wally, and he was a nice guy. A simple guy. Just wanted to work, get paid, and take care of his dog. Dog's name is Betsy. She's cute, and she loved Wally, with the boundless love a dog has for its master. But she can't love Wally anymore, because he took your job, because he thought it was a way out of the cycle he was trapped in, and I guess he was right, because he's dead. Except it's worse than that, because you're still using him, even now. Free labor, right?"

Joe advanced on Petry, his gun closer to the doctor's head.

"And you think it's okay, because *you* didn't inject him. You didn't come up with the science. You just watched it happen and stood silently by and let it."

Anna stared at the screen. The transfer was complete. "Give me the thumb drive." Petry pulled it out and handed it over.

"Now delete everything in the network drive," she said, her voice cold.

"I can't do that," said Petry.

"Yes, you can," said Anna. "And you will."

"I can't just delete everything!" said Petry. "There's fail-safes that'll stop me—"

"Then turn them off," said Joe. "And delete the backups. And the backups to the backups."

Petry turned to stare at him. "This is years of research! You can't just delete it all!"

Joe pointed the gun at him and cocked it. "If you can't delete it, I'll shoot you now. We can destroy the physical equipment with just your key."

"No, please—"

"Then delete it," said Joe. "Stop making excuses. Find a way. That's what Mr. Johnson tells me when I'm behind on orders. Find a way."

Petry stared for a second longer and then turned back to

the computer, and began typing, opening up new windows and entering passwords. Joe and Anna watched him.

"Security won't let you get away with this," said Petry. "Boggins won't let you get away with this."

"They're not here," said Anna. "Keep working."

"I'm trying," said Petry. "It's going to alert people, I can't stop it—"

"Are they here?" asked Joe.

"No," said Petry. "They're in offices on the west coast—"

"Then I don't care," said Joe.

"There," said Petry. "I've erased every trace."

"Anna, check it," said Joe. He grabbed Petry by the collar and pulled him away. Anna crouched down in front of the monitors and explored the interface.

"It's gone, as far as I can tell," said Anna. "Network drive empty. Backups empty. Cloud protection turned off."

"It's a travesty," said Petry. "So much of that is irreplaceable. It'll take years to get back where we were—"

"I hope it takes longer," said Joe. "Come on, let's go. Take us to the lab."

"Please, let me leave—"

"The labs," said Joe. "Lead."

Petry looked at him for a moment, and then walked, leading them back out. Back through the hallways, with Petry's key card leading the way.

"I don't know how you intend to destroy those labs—"

"Quiet," said Joe. Back in the hallways, Joe remembered the guards interrupting him last time. They could do it again, they could jump around the corner, and the pistol in his hand was heavy—

But then they came out into a central hallway, and he

recognized where they were, and Petry led them to where Joe had explored before. To the labs.

The room smelled like chemicals, still, and Joe rankled at the stink.

"We destroy it all," said Joe.

"These chemicals are dangerous, you can't—"

"Oh, they're dangerous?" asked Joe. He looked around the room and saw a couple of crates in the corner, with a pry bar leaning against them. "We best get rid of them."

Joe handed the gun to Anna, who held it out, pointing at Dr. Petry. Joe grabbed the pry bar and began smashing everything. He cracked computer monitors and jammed the bar through computer workstations. Smoke rose from the machines as he pierced through the electronics. Petry only watched.

Joe swept the pry bar across the vials of chemicals, across the various pieces of mixing equipment. Glass shattered, and smoke rose from the chemicals as they spread across the tables and floor, mixing.

"You're going to kill us," said Petry.

"I don't think so," said Joe. It felt good. Joe had kept his anger and rage at bay for weeks now, ever since he saw Wally behind those bars, undead, and he let it out now, as he smashed piece after piece of equipment. The pry bar rattled and shook as it crashed against computers and chemistry equipment, pieces of metal and glass shattering. Chemicals splashed across the stainless steel backdrops.

Anna and Dr. Petry watched as Joe destroyed everything he saw. Finally, there was nothing left but the larger vat in the middle of the lab, filled with the dark red liquid. It looked like gasoline.

"This is it, isn't it?" asked Joe, looking at Petry. "This is what they injected them with."

"I don't know," said Petry. "I wasn't—"

"You weren't there, I know," said Joe. "It wasn't your fault." Joe took the sharp end of the pry bar and aimed it at the center of the vat.

"It's dangerous," said Petry. "Don't do it."

Joe reared back and swung at the dark red vat of chemicals, the sharp end of the bar cracking through the thick glass. The glass splintered, but didn't break. Joe swung again.

A huge hole opened up, and the thick red liquid poured out onto the ground. It smelled terrible, like death, like rot, like the end of everything.

It poured onto the ground, and through the thin grating that covered the channel in the middle of the floor. The liquid poured down and then disappeared, only a shallow layer left in the vat.

They all watched it empty.

"Only the zombies left."

19

The creatures ambled in their cells, sorting invisible packages and taping nonexistent boxes.

"Oh god," said Anna. Joe glanced at her. She hadn't seen the zombies before, and she covered her face with her hands, trying to collect herself.

The smell was horrible, the undead rotting while they stood, pieces of flesh sloughing off the older bodies onto the ground, where it was stamped into the concrete floor.

Petry's face was a mask, but Joe saw his disgust peek through.

"We destroy them, and this is done," said Joe.

Petry shook his head.

"You're wasting your time," he said.

"What did I say about you talking?"

Petry turned and looked at him, his eyes narrowing.

"You can't kill them, you idiot," said Petry. "And none of this matters. You think you can stop Nile? Do you think this will make any difference at all?"

"Shut up," said Joe. "With all this gone, and the news breaking the story—"

"Do you think you wiped everything?" asked Petry. "You think the research is truly gone? There's more of it out there. And as soon as the story breaks, people will reverse engineer what little Nile has done, and recreate it. Bringing the dead back to life. You don't think someone else won't go poking into the same places? There's no putting the toothpaste back in the tube, there's no undoing this advancement—"

"Advancement?" asked Joe. "Look at these monsters! They're inhuman! They're rotting! You can look at these things, who were once people, who you *killed*, and say this is an advancement?"

"This is the beginning," said Petry. "Tech always gets better, especially medical tech. Think about heart transplants, about polio, about diabetes. We've gotten better and better. This will be the same. This is the future. Why do we waste the dead, when they could work for us forever?"

A heat of rage passed through Joe and he stepped forward and smashed the pistol into Petry's face, once, twice, a third time, and then Anna was in front of him, pushing him back. Petry was on the ground, his face bloody, his nose broken, his glasses shattered.

"Where's your heart?" yelled Joe. "What's wrong with you, where you can watch this happen and do nothing but stand by, and cash your paycheck?"

Petry laid on the ground, blood covering his face. He

wiped at the blood leaking from his nose.

"Do you think there's no one else working on this? Do you think that Microsoft wouldn't do it? Or Walmart? Or Starbucks? Or Apple?" Petry pushed himself to his feet. "Of course they would. Does it matter if I object? Does it change anything?" He spit out a wad of blood. "No. It changes nothing."

Joe only stared at him, anger still simmering

He walked over to the cell with Wally in it. Wally stood against one wall, staring straight ahead, his hands moving, doing now in death what he did tirelessly in life.

Wally stared ahead with unblinking eyes, with no thought, no recognition. There was nothing in there anymore, nothing but the few programmed actions Nile did their best to instill in the creature.

His death was a tragedy, horrific, but Wally was better off dead than whatever state this was.

Joe raised his pistol and pointed it at Wally's head, between the bars of the cell.

Do it, Joe. You're doing him a mercy, by killing him here. Shoot him, once in the head. Stop this.

Joe stared at Wally. He took a deep breath, closed his eyes, opened them, aimed carefully, and shot.

BANG

The pistol fired, the loud shot echoing in the room, Joe's ears ringing.

But Wally still stood.

Joe blinked. Had he missed?

No, he hadn't missed.

Wally turned, in reaction to the shot, and Joe saw both the entry and exit wound, the entry wound a relatively small bloody circle, but the exit wound was ghastly, a huge chunk of bone and flesh missing, with Wally's partially destroyed, rotting brain leaking from inside. Joe swallowed his disgust down.

Wally seemed confused now, as confused as these creatures could be, the head trauma leaving him looking for something—perhaps the source of the damage. Did they still feel pain?

Joe didn't know. But Wally still stood, still moved. The headshot had done nothing except superficial damage.

No, it had to kill them. He must have missed the brain, somehow—

He raised the gun again. A second shot would do it.

"You don't listen," said Petry, from behind him. "You're wasting your time."

"You can't stop me."

"I don't need to do anything to stop you," said Dr. Petry. "Why do you think destroying the brain will do anything?"

Joe almost answered, but said nothing.

Because it works in the movies.

"This isn't Night of the Living Dead," said Petry. "The tissue was dead. All of it, including the brain. Why would destroying it again stop them?"

"It's not possible for them to endure forever," said Anna. "Enough trauma, and anything will die."

"They'll rot, eventually," said Petry. "But under a microscope, even the putrescent flesh still has activity."

"What the fuck," said Joe.

"The wonder of the science," said Petry. "With enough refinement, we can cure death. And you want to destroy all this work—"

Joe turned then, away from the creatures, back to Petry. Petry's face was covered in blood from Joe's pistol whipping, and Joe raised the pistol again to Petry's head, putting the barrel to his temple.

"You won't survive it, though," said Joe. "You're still human. You can still die."

"Joe, don't—"

"Why not, Anna?" asked Joe. "He's a part of it. He helped. Maybe he didn't inject them, but he knew. He supported it. He got his paycheck."

"Joe, you're not a killer," said Anna. "Please, let's just go. We've done what we can."

"He'll know our faces, Anna," said Joe. "He'll rat us out. We'll go to prison."

"We didn't discuss this—"

Joe looked at Anna. "He's part of the problem, Anna. He's no different from any of the others—"

Anna stared back. "Joe, we can't—"

The door to the lab opened, interrupting her.

"We heard something from—" said Gary, followed by the second guard. They saw Joe with his pistol drawn, and immediately drew their own guns. Joe moved behind Petry, pulling the doctor close, holding the gun to his head, using him as a shield. Anna threw up her arms.

Fuck. The thumb drive. They can't have it.

Joe snaked fingers into his pocket, grabbed the drive, and slid it into his mouth. He didn't know if it would fit down his throat.

"Please, don't shoot, he's gone crazy, he has a gun," said Anna, moving away. Joe coated the drive with all the saliva he had, and swallowed. It stuck, just for a moment, and then it went down.

"Back away, Dr. Marshall," said Gary. "Dr. Petry, are you okay?"

"No, I'm not okay," said Petry. "My nose is broken. This man has destroyed research. Stop him!"

"Shut your mouth," said Joe, to Petry. He held the gun firm against his head. "They're keeping fucking zombies, Gary. You okay with that?"

"Above my pay grade," said Gary, staring at Joe. "You've got to let him go—John, was it?"

"I'm not letting him go unless I get to go free," said Joe. "Otherwise he dies with me."

"Whoa whoa whoa," said Gary. "No one has to die." The second security guard circled Joe.

"Hey, Muttley, stay next to Gary, or Petry eats a bullet," said Joe. The second guard froze. The zombies started making more noise, riled up by the gunshot and all the commotion. They pushed to the front of their cells, dozens of creatures banging against the metal rails of their doors. They reached out in fury, anger unrestrained.

"You're making them upset," said Gary.

"Oh, am I?" asked Joe. "Oh no, the poor zombies. How will they live with the stress?"

"Petry's just a scientist," said Gary. "Let him go. This doesn't have to end in violence."

Joe caught movement in his periphery. Anna crept slowly. Neither of the guards were looking at her. They had assumed her a victim as well. She was moving toward the control panel for the cells.

"You're going to get us out of here," said Joe. "And then I'll let him go."

"Sounds good," said Gary, his eyes doing his best to convince Joe. They wouldn't let him out of here. They just wanted away from the zombies, in a place where the two guards had more of an upper hand.

"Shoot him," said Petry. Joe pushed the gun hard into his temple.

"Hey hey hey," said Gary. "Calm down, Dr. Petry. We'll get you out of this." The guards' eyes were only on him. They had forgotten about Anna. And she had sidled over to the control panel. It was the only chance they had to get out of here. Let the creatures loose and get out in the chaos.

Joe took a deep breath. His heart was pumping hard in his chest. He glanced at Anna. She was ready and looked at him.

"Hit it," he said, and then Anna opened the cells, all at once.

The doors clanked open, and the zombies, already agitated, stumbled their way out of their cells. There were dozens of them, and they pushed their way out.

"What the fuck—" yelled Gary, and then he and the other guard turned to the swarm heading toward them. Anna was already running to the door, and Gary grabbed for her and she tripped.

Joe turned to run, but then Petry grabbed at him, trying to get his pistol. Joe pulled hard, to get the gun away, but he had let down his guard, and Petry had both hands on Joe's wrist. He pulled hard with his whole body, and the pistol went flying. Petry fell backwards on the ground without the pistol.

Gary and the second guard fired a handful of shots at the creatures as they moved, but nothing worked, and they turned to run. The second guard grabbed Anna, picking her off the ground, and they ran. The creatures were mindless, filled with anger, and they moved quickly, even as they stumbled on unsteady and unsure legs. They would surround him in a second, and he went to run, but Petry grabbed his ankle from the ground.

"You sonofa—" said Petry, growling. He squeezed Joe's ankle, but Joe kicked at his face, once, twice, and he hit Petry's already broken nose and Petry let go, the pain too much.

Joe ran, the small horde almost around them. He sprinted to the door, just behind Anna and the second guard. Joe hurried, feeling the rotted breath of the zombies behind him, and then they were through the door. He turned, glanced back, the guards already shutting it.

Petry was still on the ground, surrounded by the creatures. They saw something alive, and they were filled with rage, filled with anger.

Anger at the audacity of them to be alive, when the creatures no longer were.

Petry looked up at Joe, his eyes full of hopelessness and terror, and then the zombies tore him apart.

They sank their gnarled hands into Petry's soft flesh, and pulled. The creatures weren't hungry. They weren't after brains. They only wanted to destroy the living.

And then the two guards slammed the door shut, the electronic lock buzzing shut.

"Put your fucking hands up," said Gary, his gun pulled on Anna and Joe. Joe stared at him and put them up slowly.

Petry screamed from beyond the door. He screamed and screamed, until his throat was ripped from him.

20

Joe sat in a cramped holding cell, with a toilet in the corner and a tiny cot. He sat on it, waiting. Gary and Muttley had marched them through more hallways to this area at gunpoint. Without his pistol, Joe had little recourse.

Anna was in another cell, and the guards had disappeared. Joe had yelled after them, but they hadn't responded. That was hours ago.

The adrenaline had worn off, of the brief crisis with the guards, of narrowly escaping the zombies, of the dead ripping Dr. Petry apart. Joe had been so angry at him, and had been ready to kill him, ready to shoot him. But after seeing him ripped apart, he realized he didn't want anyone to die. Too many had died already.

Except for those in charge at Nile. They deserved worse

than death.

But Joe was tired now. It was the middle of the night, but he didn't know when exactly. Gary had confiscated their phones, taken everything. He desperately wanted to sleep, but he was afraid to let down his guard.

Not that it mattered.

"Anna, you awake?" asked Joe.

"Yes," she said. She was right next door. Joe had seen three cells. He didn't know why Nile needed holding cells, but who knows what else they had hidden here. How many other people had been in this holding cell?

"We're fucked, aren't we?"

"Probably," said Anna.

"What the hell is taking so long? Would have thought the police would be here by now."

"They're not calling the police," said Anna. "If there was any question of it before, it's not one anymore. Nile won't let the police handle this. I imagine they're waking people up, and deciding what to do, and how to do it. They've suffered a loss, and now they have the two people responsible for it."

"Are they going to kill us?"

"Maybe," said Anna, her voice dry. "Probably depends on what we say, and what we do when they interrogate us."

"At least we got the bastards," said Joe. "We did some damage."

"Did we?"

"We wiped their research," said Joe. "We destroyed their equipment." He didn't say anything about the thumb drive. Had she seen him swallow it? They had to get it out of here.

Anna didn't answer. The thought of Petry screaming as he was ripped apart entered his mind. Screaming as hard as he could, the zombies' ragged, rotting hands plunging through his skin and ripping his guts out. Would he come back, too? Would the chemical infect him as well, or would he stay blessedly dead? Joe pictured the ripped apart pieces of Petry pulling themselves along the floor of the lab, and then he forced the thought out of his mind. Would Nile continue on as normal, without Anna on the team? Would they dispose of them and then return to business as usual?

Or would the two of them join the ranks of the undead?

"Gary!" yelled Joe, raising his voice.

There was no response. Joe only saw a thin hallway leading away from his cell, but couldn't even see the door that had led them to this area.

"Gary!" yelled Joe, again.

"He's not going to answer—" started Anna, and then Joe heard a door creak open.

"Stop yelling," said Gary, walking down the hallway until he stood in front of Joe's cell. Gary had collected himself.

"We've been here for hours," said Joe. "This is kidnapping, illegal detainment. Either turn us over to the police or let us go."

Gary stared at Joe. "We're following procedure."

"Procedure dictates that you illegally detain both Anna and I for hours—"

"You trespassed, you destroyed files and equipment, you committed manslaughter—"

"The zombies killed Dr. Petry, not us!"

"You let them out," said Gary. "They weren't hurting anyone while they were still in their cells."

"Will you listen to yourself? They're fucking zombies, Gary! Those used to be my co-workers, and Nile fucking killed them, and you're just staring at me, blindly reciting procedure! How the hell do you sleep at night?"

Gary stared at him blankly. "Procedure says to inform Mr. Boggins of what happened, and we did that. He said he'd take care of everything else, and for us to hold you until he arrived."

"You don't care?" asked Joe. "You don't care that all those people were killed by the company you work for? That you're helping them cover it up?"

"It's not my problem."

"It will be," said Joe. "You don't think it's weird that you're not supposed to call the police, Gary? That Boggins is going to take care of it all?"

"It's not my problem,."

"You're not the police," said Joe. "You can't hold us like this."

"Nile will do the right thing—"

"Aren't you worried you'll be the next target?"

"I don't know what you're talking about—"

"You think you're not disposable?" asked Joe. He stared into Gary's eyes, and they wavered, just for a second. "You're just some guard, Gary. You and Muttley both. You probably don't get paid anymore than I do, working over in the fulfillment center."

"His name is Sean. What's your point?"

"You never worry about how much you know?" asked Joe. "A lot of responsibility, with the amount of Nile's dirt you know. Maybe one day Boggins or whoever decides you're too much of a risk, and you get thrown into one of those cells, and the zombies take care of you."

"I signed an NDA, when I joined up, I wouldn't—"

"Yeah, yeah," said Joe. "I'm sure Boggins won't do anything, as long as you honor your NDA."

"I'm doing my job," said Gary. "Please don't yell anymore."

"Remember this conversation when you're up against the wall, Gary," said Joe. "Because it'll be you next."

Gary only stared at him for a moment longer and then walked away. Anna said nothing.

Joe sat back on the cot.

"Sorry, Wally," said Joe, quietly, to himself. They had tried, and now he was locked in this cell. He thought to his mom. What would she do, after Joe disappeared? What would Helen do? Would Helen raise a fuss? Would she come after him?

He didn't know. It had seemed so sure. He leaned back and closed his eyes. The cot wasn't that comfortable, but he was tired, and resting his eyes felt great—

We only have each other.

Joe opened his eyes. He sat in Wally's living room. Wally sat on the couch, covered in shadow.

"I know, Wally, I know," said Joe. "What you said—it really affected me. I wanted to do right by you."

"Do right by me?" asked Wally. Betsy sat on his lap, sleeping, and Wally pet her, absentmindedly. "How did you plan to do that? By fucking up your stupid mission? Fucking it up like you've fucked up everything else in your life?"

"Wally—"

"It seems like there's only one common denominator between all your fuck-ups, Joe, and that's you. You're the shared bingo space. Maybe it's not the system's fault, maybe it's not capitalism's fault, maybe it's your fault!"

"Wally, what's going on—"

Wally leaned forward, and blood filled his eyes, with black streaks running through them.

"You blame everything but yourself, Joe. You blame some big company, like it's their fault that you're a failure! That your mother bled herself to the bone raising you, of providing everything you ever needed, and you couldn't take the baton and run with it when her body ran down. You dropped out of college, you got fired from every job you've ever had, you've *failed* her—"

Joe's heart pounded hard, and he wanted to run, but he couldn't move, he was frozen in place, and Wally stared at him with his red eyes, veins protruding from his skin, and the bullet wound was there, and half of Wally's face was gone, blown out by Joe's pistol—

"You tried to kill me," said Wally. "But you failed. Failed again, Joe. Is there anything you *can* do?" Betsy jumped up and sprinted away, and Joe reached for her, but couldn't move—

Please, help, please, someone—

"Ah, I know," said Wally. "There's something you can do. You can die." Wally leapt off the couch with incredible quickness, his arms outstretched, his hands clawed, and they plunged into Joe's stomach, and he felt Wally's fingers rip at his flesh, his guts being ripped from inside him, his intestines tumbling out of him, strings of sausages wrapped up in Wally's fingers, and he pulled, and pulled, and more and more came out of him—

"Wake up, Mr. Amery," boomed a voice, and Joe's eyes bolted open, and he yelled, the sound pulled from him.

He was still in the cell. He had nodded off, his body finally succumbing to the exhaustion. His heart thumped in his chest, and his hands went to his stomach instinctively, wanting to put himself back inside himself—

But then he realized where he was, and the voice that woke him up. He looked to his cell door. He recognized the man standing on the other side of it.

Boggins.

Boggins stood there, with two men, dressed in all black tactical gear, each holding an assault rifle. They wore masks over their faces.

"Mr. Amery," said Boggins. "It's time we talked."

21

Boggins stared at Joe with those awful eyes. They stared at Joe, considered him. It felt like an alien sat behind those eyes.

Maybe one did.

But Boggins didn't seem as unearthly as he had when Joe first met him. Cracks had formed in the veneer. His face sagged, and his eyes betrayed weariness. Maybe from receiving a call in the middle of the night that his research department had been attacked.

They sat in an interrogation room. Somewhere in the facility.

"I suspected," said Boggins, finally, staring at Joe. The two armed men stood behind him, their eyes shielded by dark sunglasses. The assault rifles they carried were slung around their shoulders, but their fingers were never far from the trigger. They wore no insignia on their tactical gear or body armor. It was all black. They weren't police or government. They were mercenaries hired by Nile. Or maybe Nile's own wetworks. Joe didn't know, but he knew they could kill him in a moment if they wanted. "I suspected, after you turned down the job offer."

Joe stared at him. Joe was exhausted. They had held him for hours, but Joe had no idea of what time it actually was. They had gone into the building before midnight, but it surely was almost dawn by now. Or past? Joe didn't know. Would workers at the fulfillment center be showing up for the first shift?

"Who told you?" asked Boggins.

"No one told me anything," said Joe.

"Please, Mr. Amery," said Boggins. "You and Dr. Marshall just stumbled upon all this tonight? I highly doubt that."

"Your security is shit," said Joe. "Anna only had to threaten calling you, and security caved."

"Yes," said Boggins. He took a deep breath. "Believe me, I'm aware. It's an oversight that won't be repeated. But you had Dr. Petry's key card. How did you get it?"

Joe stared at him. He said nothing.

"Please, Mr. Amery," said Boggins. "I don't want to beat you, but these men will do it without hesitation. Do you need more pain in your life? Because not answering my questions will only give you more."

Joe stared into his eyes. He exhaled.

"Petry is dead, so I can't ask him anything. But he was loyal. He wouldn't be a part of your plot, whatever it is," said

Boggins.

Joe said nothing.

"Fine, have it your way. Hawkins, break his arm." The man on the right of Boggins came forward. Joe still couldn't see his eyes.

"I took it from him," said Joe. "After I pointed a gun at him."

Boggins raised his hand, and Hawkins stepped back to the wall.

"See, that wasn't so hard," said Boggins. "Why was he here so late, though? He's an early riser."

"He liked Anna," said Joe. "At least that's what she said. She used it to her advantage. Asked for help, late at night. Petry fell for it. He had access to everything."

"Well, not everything." Boggins took a deep breath, and exhaled through his nose. "You fucked us, Joe. We had a good setup here. We were making actual progress. And now, now it's gone."

"Good," said Joe. Boggins' eyes sparked with a brief anger.

"Good?" asked Boggins. Boggins' calm facade cracked for the first time. He actually appeared human, for once. His lip sneered and then returned to normal. "You have no idea what you've done. Do you know how long it's taken us to get to this point? Do you understand the costs over the years? They've been astronomical. We finally had a breakthrough, and you step in and smash everything we've built like a child at the beach, destroying a sand castle. Petry is dead. He was an excellent scientist, a good man—"

"Go fuck yourself," said Joe.

"How dare—"

"Go fuck yourself," said Joe, staring into Boggins' eyes. He took a deep breath. "You believe it, too. That's the worst thing with you fucks. Sometimes, I can tell, you know, when they don't really believe it. Petry, I'll give him that. He didn't really believe. Petry saw a paycheck, and the steps to achieve it. He reckoned if it wasn't him, it'd be someone else. And he wasn't wrong. It'd be some other stupid ass doctor dead, ripped apart by those things, if he had chosen another path."

Boggins only stared at him.

"He didn't think what you were doing was right, or good. Maybe he told himself that whenever the guilt popped back up. Whenever one of those things looked him in the eye, and he remembered what they once were. But deep down, he didn't believe that Nile had any altruistic intent. They wanted to develop tech that would save them money. Period. But you—you believe. You believe in this horror. You believe that sacrificing workers like kindling on a fire is for the best, not because you believe it's altruistic, but because you think finding a new way to save the company money is good, is moral, is right. Your mind is rotted to the core, and everyone above you in the company thinks the exact same way."

"We brought people back to life," said Boggins, his voice calm, his face matching. The brief emotion had been tamped down.

"You killed them, you piece of shit," said Joe. "They didn't need to be brought back to life. But a zombie worker is more valuable to you than a human one."

"You want a utopia?" asked Boggins. "How do you think we get there? You want a future where no one works? What do you think that looks like? Automation can only get us so far. The machines aren't going to save us. They're too stupid, and far too slow to learn. Humanity is still better at every job." Boggins shook his head. "But they're costly. They need too much. They need to eat, and drink, and piss, and shit, and they need to get paid, and they need to be *happy*. The dead—the dead need nothing. They will do what they're taught to do, forever."

"They rot," said Joe. "Petry said—"

"They rot *now*," said Boggins. "With more time, and more experiments, we'll stop that too. And we won't kill people, not after we've gotten the technology right. People will sell their dead to us, and be paid handsomely. People die every day, Mr. Amery. And soon, there will be an army of workers who will work forever, and the living will benefit." Boggins smiled, as wide as Joe had seen.

"You mean *you* will benefit. Nile, and Apple, and the people who own them, and run them. You'll have less workers to pay, and better efficiency from the dead who work for you. But I won't benefit. I'll be fighting with the rest of us over what jobs are left. Because it's a lie I've been told my whole life. About how machines are going to save us. How automation is going to save us. It isn't. It's going to be used to crush me more efficiently." Joe narrowed his eyes. "Well, it would have. But now it's gone. Deleted. Destroyed."

"You did destroy a lot of our work," said Boggins. "But it won't matter. We'll pivot. We'll make it work. And honestly, Mr. Amery, you've done us a favor. Breaking the news to the public was always our biggest concern. How do we spin the breakthrough? How do we make people understand? The response with tests have always been shock and horror, and that's no good. We always tried to soften it, and put all the benefits front and center, but people saw the creatures, and they recoiled. They couldn't get past it."

"What the hell are you talking about?" asked Joe.

"But we never thought to front load all that horror," said Boggins. "It makes sense, though, right? Present them as they are. Awful, rotting things. But then, come in with a silver lining afterward. Yes, these things exist. Yes, they're horrible. But—we can use them. We can make our world better with them."

Joe only stared. "What the fuck are you saying?"

Boggins stared at him with a smirk. "What exactly do you think you dumped down the drain, back in the lab?"

Joe's mind went back to when they destroyed the lab. He punched a massive hole in the vat, holding that dark red liquid. It stank as it ran into the floor, through the grate.

"And Mr. Amery, where exactly do you think that liquid went?"

A dark spike of ice speared through Joe's heart. He couldn't breathe.

"Let me fill you in," said Boggins, the smirk still there. "You've been open about your plans. I'll return the favor. The chemical you dumped is the result of thousands of hours of testing and research. It brings the dead back to life. But it is also incredibly, incredibly toxic. When we injected it into the subjects, we had to dilute it an absurd amount. Hell, we had to include some chemicals in the mix that *neutralized* the reagent to make it weaker. But in that vat, the one you dumped down the drains? Pure. Pure death. And those drains lead right to a creek that feeds the river, that feeds the aquifer that the whole town drinks from."

"We have to do something, we have to stop it—" Joe rose

from his seat. The two men with rifles immediately stepped forward.

"Why don't you calm down, Mr. Amery?" asked Boggins. "There's nothing we can do. Especially anymore."

"What do you mean? We have to warn people!"

"Please, Mr. Amery. You don't need to raise your voice. We've already done the math. When I got the call, about what you've done. I talked to those who make the decisions, and like I said, we did the math." Boggins looked at his watch. "It's been about twelve hours since you've dumped that chemical down the drain. I was in a rush at first, you know, after I heard what you and Dr. Marshall did. But then we realized that this could benefit us. So I took my time. I gathered the boys here, and we came, and got a sitrep. But we *took our time*. Gave the chemical enough time to work its way through Springfield's admittedly aging water utilities. It's about 10 AM, if you were wondering. Which is just enough time for everyone to wake up. To brush their teeth. To take a shower. To drink a glass of water. All of it poisoned. Even diluted in Springfield's water system, that chemical is deadly. Soon, all those people will be dead."

Boggins stared at him, the smirk still lingering.

"And then, Mr. Amery, they will come back."

22

"You're lying."

Joe stared at Boggins, his eyes set on Boggins' inscrutable face. Boggins stared back.

"It'll be in the water for years, Joe. Nothing can be done about it at this point. Too late to intercede, and it'll seep into the groundwater for generations. Springfield is dead. Or undead, if you prefer."

"You son of a bitch—" Joe's hands squeezed into fists. He'd jump over the table, and throttle Boggins, he'd pound him into paste—

"Calm down now, Mr. Amery. Like I said, nothing can be done about it now," said Boggins. "Why do you think it took so long for me to talk to you?"

Joe thought to Helen. To his mother. Both used Springfield water. They would die, he had to do something, had to get to them. Had to call them, tell them not to drink the water. He stood up, breathing hard. The two guards stepped forward, their rifles up in a moment, both pointing at him. One quick pull and he would die, high caliber bullets ripping him apart.

"Please sit down, Mr. Amery," said Boggins.

He sat down. Tears welled in the corners of his eyes, and he blinked hard, trying to force them back. He couldn't break down, not now. Joe wouldn't, not in front of Boggins. Boggins didn't deserve his tears.

"I should be thanking you, Mr. Amery," said Boggins. "You've given us a solution to the problem. You've given us a way out, even if it's not entirely ideal."

"You won't get away with this."

"We won't?"

"You think no one will notice a town overrun by zombies?" asked Joe. "You think the government won't do anything? They'll realize who's responsible, and the public will explode. They'll see what I've seen, and even Nile can't withstand that kind of publicity. The President will do something, and Nile will be fucked."

Boggins smiled then, staring at Joe, confused, and then laughed, an alien sound coming from that face. Boggins caught himself, and tamped the smile back down.

"I'm sorry, Mr. Amery, you'll have to excuse me," said Boggins, ashamed of his own emotion. "I just thought—"

"You thought what?"

"I thought you understood," said Boggins. "I really thought you did." He took a deep breath. "Oh well, it doesn't change anything."

"What are you talking about? Understood what?"

"It's my fault, really," said Boggins. "I assumed. I assumed you were smarter than you are."

"Go fuck yourself."

"Oh, Mr. Amery, no need for that," said Boggins. He stared, his face plain again, his eyes cold. "Do you really think Nile would undertake something like this without the government's knowledge? Without its blessing?"

Of course, Joe. Of course.

"Nile is the largest company on Earth, Mr. Amery," said Boggins. "And certainly has a large impact on the US government's policies, around business, certainly, but about everything, honestly. Now think to yourself. Ask yourself. A creature like those we have here. Dead, for all intents and purposes. Unthinking. Needs no food, no water, no sleep. Can do simple tasks. Like holding and firing a gun, let's say. And most importantly, is unkillable. Can take infinite damage, and never hurt, and never stop, not until they are obliterated. Will fight until they literally can't anymore. Do you think that would have value for the US military?"

"You monster."

"The government is highly invested in our research," said Boggins. "Nothing official, obviously. But the people who need to know, know, and know well our progress. There's already been communication about what's happening here in Springfield. There will be great anger, and great shock, about what's happened. And people will try and get to the bottom of it. It'll be hard, at first, reckoning with all the deaths, but soon after, Nile will fund exploratory missions into Springfield. After some time, they will become normal. It's shocking how much the public will accept, as long as they are given time to get used to it. And once they do, we reveal what we've discovered. The chemical. The ability of the undead to work for us. And they'll accept it as a fact of life. Sure, Springfield will be unlivable for generations, but it's a small price. The creatures will be reined in, with time. They'll rot, and die, and then the town will be the perfect place to build a full research lab. Out in the open. No more need for secrecy."

Joe exhaled through his nose, trying to control his anger. He stared at Boggins, burning a hole through him with his eyes.

"Mr. Amery, I do not understand your anger," said Boggins. "I'm only following orders. I did not choose to pursue this technology, or to ally ourselves with the US military. I don't know why you want to blame me. In fact, this was all contained. Isolated in this lab. Not a danger to any of the public. But you had to make a statement. You had to do the right thing. Well, this is the end result. More death. More suffering."

"I won't let you get away with this," said Joe. "Nile will pay. Every single one of you, that let this happen. That let these people die—"

"No, you won't," said Boggins.

"You fucking piece of shit," said Joe. "They'll find out, they'll know, I'll make sure of it—"

"You'll do no such thing," said Boggins. "In a couple hours, you, Dr. Marshall, and the rest of the undead here will be destroyed, and your bodies burned. You've destroyed all evidence of our involvement. No one will know, and we will pick up the pieces, put our research back together, and use the situation to our advantage. Take him back to his cell." Boggins got up, and looked at him a final time. "Good-bye, Mr. Amery."

23

"I won't allow it," Mom said.

She was still in her uniform, washing dishes over their small sink. She always washed dishes when she got upset, Joe didn't know why. Maybe it was just to keep her hands busy.

"Mom, you're being crazy," said Joe.

"I'm not being crazy," she said. "You didn't even talk this over with me. You just went ahead and did it."

"I wanted to surprise you! I thought you'd be happy!" he said, his voice raising. He didn't want to yell, hated yelling at his mom, but she was making it hard.

Joe stared at the back of her head. She wouldn't turn around, scrubbing the dishes, up to her elbows in the brackish water. He took a breath.

"I thought you'd be happy that I got a job."

He *had* wanted it to be a surprise. The local grocery store was hiring, part time, for bag boys and cart attendants, and Joe had thought about it, and applied. He'd gotten the job with little trouble. It was a job meant for teenagers like him and had no requirements aside from a commitment to show up on time and put up with the minimum wage pay. And he would, because it was the only place in town that would hire a fifteen-year-old.

He started tomorrow.

"Mom, please," he said, when she didn't answer. "Please talk to me."

Her shoulders slumped, and she pulled her hands from the water, and grabbed a spare towel, drying herself off, finally facing him.

Her eyes met his, and they were tired. And sad.

"I don't understand," he said. "I thought you'd be happy."

"You're fifteen," she said, looking at him. "Fifteen years old. A kid."

"I'm not a kid—"

"Yes, you are," she said. "I know that everything around you is telling you that you're grown up now. That in a couple years you'll be out of high school, and ready to face the world, and that you're already making decisions that will shape your whole life. Doing the right things now, in high school, that will get you into college, and then deciding there what the shape of the rest of your life will be."

She put the towel down. She approached him and took his hands in hers.

"But you're still a kid," she said. "And I know I've always said that. That you'll always be my little boy. But even at fifteen—you shouldn't have a job."

"I just wanted to help," he said, his voice quiet.

"Oh, Joe—"

"I've watched you work yourself to death, Mom. Ever since Dad passed, you've driven yourself into the ground to make sure that we had everything we needed. That *I* had everything *I* needed. And plenty of things I didn't need, only wanted. Even now. And now, now I can help. I can chip in. I wanted to help pay some bills, to help you put more into savings—"

"It's not your responsibility," she said.

"Mom—"

"My parents made me pay rent," she said. "Your Dad did too, when he was a kid. It was something we had in common, when we first started dating. We both resented it."

"You never told me."

"Because it was never an expectation," she said. "I didn't have you to have another little worker in the house. I had you because I wanted to give you a better life than the one I had. Where you didn't have to devote yourself to a job before you even knew who you were."

She squeezed his hands.

"Do you *want* to have a job?" she asked. "Or would you rather hang out with your friends after school? Or join a club? Or a sports team? Or learn guitar?"

"I want to help you," said Joe. "I want to contribute."

"You can contribute by having fun," said Mom. "By enjoying your childhood. Because soon enough, all of that will be behind you."

"I—"

"Keep the job if you want it," she said. "But I won't take

your money. I'll shoulder the burden. I've done it for this long. Okay?"

"Okay," he said. She let go of his hands and then hugged him.

"I love you," she said.

"I love you, too."

24

They returned Joe to his cell. The mercs took Anna to speak to Boggins after him, but he had no chance to warn her about the news Boggins would assuredly tell her.

There was one other difference upon his return to his cell. The third cell, formerly empty, was now occupied. The two security guards sat inside, Gary and Sean.

The mercs left Joe in his cell and then left.

Joe had thought to attack the mercs while they took him back to his cell, but he had never been a good fighter, and they were both armed, bigger than him, and presumably skilled in hand to hand combat. He was angry, but he wasn't delirious.

But he hadn't surrendered to his fate, not yet. The thumb drive was still in him, working its way through his guts, and he would be out of this facility by the time it worked through him. He could still save Helen, could still save his mom. There was a chance they hadn't been infected, hadn't drank any city water.

Helen only drank sparkling water, and she sometimes skipped showers in the morning. His mother drank the diet green tea from the store and often slept in. He just had to get out of here without being shot and burned.

But for now, he was alone in his cell. But not completely alone.

"Hey, Gary," said Joe, yelling over to their cell. He waited a beat, but there was no response.

"Gary, you there?" he asked again.

"What do you want?" asked Gary, yelling back.

"What happened?" asked Joe. "Why are you in the cell?" He tried to keep his voice level. He wanted to rub it in Gary's face. Gary was in the cell for the same reason he and Anna were. They couldn't be allowed to live with the knowledge they had. They would be killed, just like Joe and Anna, and all the undead.

But Joe needed them. If he was going to leave this place alive, he would need allies.

There was another long pause, and Joe thought Gary wouldn't answer.

But then his voice came. "They said they need to keep us here, until the local authorities are informed about everything," said Gary. His voice sounded unsure.

"In a cell?" asked Joe. "Why couldn't they just let you wait in the common area? Or at your desks?"

"They—they said it was procedure, and they had to follow it," said Gary. "Same reason they had to take our phones, and our guns, and our ID—"

"They're going to kill us, Gary," said Joe, interrupting him.

"No, they're not," said Gary. "Me and Sean just have to wait, and once everything's squared away, they'll let us out."

"I just talked to Boggins, Gary," said Joe. "That shit's in the drinking water. It's turning Springfield into zombie town, and that's exactly what Boggins and Nile want. They want zombies to become a known entity, so they can profit from them without having to hide it."

"That's impossible," said Gary. "They wouldn't let that happen, they wouldn't—"

"It's happening right now," said Joe. "Actually, it's happened, already. But we're in the way. We know the truth. And once Boggins gets what he can out of Anna, he's going to get his soldiers to lead us out of here, shoot us, and then burn our bodies, along with the zombies here in the facility. Erase the last bit of evidence that connects this to Nile, and then they're free to use it without the PR hit."

"You did this, not us," said Gary. "We didn't do anything but our jobs. They'll let us out. You'll see."

"Gary, they're going to kill us," said Joe. "But we don't have to just sit here and take it. I don't know what they'll do, or where they'll take us, but you know the facility better than they do. With all four of us working together, we have a chance. You, me, Anna, Sean. We *can* get out of here."

"This won't work on me," said Gary. "You're trying to get out of this, and it won't work. They're going to take you and Dr. Marshall, but me and Sean, we're home free. You're making all this—"

"Gary, they're going to kill us!" yelled Joe. "Sean, you

hear me, over there? Are you going to just sit there and let it happen? If we don't come up with a plan, they're going to march us out of here, line us up against a wall, and that'll be the end of it—"

The door opened again.

"Shut the fuck up, all of you," said a stern voice. One of the mercs. "I hear you again and I'll beat the piss out of you." The door shut, the merc leaving them alone again.

"Sounds like you're a prisoner, Gary," said Joe, finally, his voice just loud enough for them to hear. But Joe left it at that. He didn't want to endanger them any further, and wouldn't be able to escape if he was half-crippled from a beating.

Anna was gone for quite a while, and a persistent thought inched its way into his mind, and it wouldn't go away. It was the thing that Joe had, the thumb drive, with all info needed to bury Nile.

But Anna knew he had it. Had seen him swallow it. She had been on board with their plan, had even laid the groundwork for it.

But—would she still keep her fortitude when her life was threatened? When she had leverage to keep herself alive?

She could use that thumb drive as leverage. Tell Boggins where it was, as long as he spared her.

Would he? Joe didn't think so, and he even thought Anna would see through any promises Boggins made. But if she thought she was going to die—desperate people do desperate things. And could even talk themselves into dumb things.

The minutes crawled by, and Joe's stomach ached. Was it from the thumb drive? Or from the thought that Anna was betraying him as he waited to be shot, his body burned, while his home turned into an undead nightmare?

There were no more words from either Gary or Sean, and without a clock, Joe had no idea how much time had passed. He could only imagine the chaos enveloping his town as people died, and then came back. His mother, opening the door to the common area of her nursing home, and one of her former friends, now turned a zombie, sprinting at her, and ripping her apart with its bare hands—

You can't think about that now. You need to get out. Focus everything on that.

After what seemed like an eternity, the mercs came back, with Anna in tow. Her face was unreadable, her eyes flicking to him, meeting his gaze for a moment, and then away. He couldn't read her.

They didn't take her back to her cell, instead, opening up both the cells for both him, and Gary and Sean. The mercs had multiplied, the two who'd been with Boggins joined by six more. Was that all of them?

Joe didn't know. It might be. They wouldn't need a big team, if they were well armed. And they were all well armed, each carrying a side arm and the same assault rifle. Joe wasn't a gun guy, but he didn't need to know the specs on the weapons to know they would kill him.

"Let's go," said Hawkins. He didn't point with the gun, not yet, but he would, if they resisted.

Hawkins and one other walked in front of them, while the rest moved behind. They were silent.

Joe felt his shoulders and back tighten. A bullet could come at any time. He would have to move quickly when he saw an opportunity. He reached over and squeezed Anna's hand, quickly, once. She looked at him, and he looked back, trying to intimate he had a plan, even if the plan was to not go easily.

They moved through unfamiliar hallways out of the holding area, past where they had spoken to Boggins. The mercs walked with purpose.

"Where are we going?" asked Gary. "What's going on?"

"Shut up," said Hawkins.

"We didn't do anything—"

One of the mercs behind them stepped up and clubbed Gary in the back with the butt of his rifle, knocking him to the ground.

"Shut the fuck up," he said, his voice firm. Gary grunted with pain, and looked up at him with anger in his eyes that turned to fear in a moment. The merc could have killed him if he hit him in the neck. Gary's eyes went to Joe's quickly, but then he was back up, and they were moving again.

As they moved, Joe recognized where they were now. It became apparent where they were taking them.

They were heading toward the zombies.

Boggins waited for them outside of the zombie's holding area, in the lab that Joe and Anna had destroyed.

The mercs herded them into the center of the room, in between the maze of desks and chairs, in the midst of the offices of the scientists who had worked there. The leader of the mercs, Hawkins, stood next to Boggins, and the rest of the mercs fell into line, standing between them and the exit. They all carried their rifles, their hands cradling the weapons.

Boggins stared at them for a moment.

"Hawkins, when you're ready," he said.

Fuck.

It was now or never, and Joe's eyes went to the steel door that held back three dozen zombies. It was his only chance. If he could release them, it would be chaos, and it would give him and Anna a chance.

"Ready," said Hawkins. The men raised their rifles. "Aim—"

"Wait, wait, wait!" yelled Anna, talking to Boggins. "Your research—it isn't destroyed. Not completely. We still have a copy."

"Hold," said Boggins. He stared at Anna. "Where is it?"

Anna took a step forward, distancing herself from the rest of them.

"I'll tell you, if you promise to let us live," said Anna.

"Anna—" started Joe.

"We can't do anything dead, Joe," said Anna, quickly. She glanced back at him, and winked, a small blink of her right eye. Whatever she was doing, she had some sort of plan.

She looked back at Boggins. "You let us live, and I'll give you the copy. All your research."

"Deal," said Boggins. "Where is it?"

"It's—"

"Anna, he'll shoot us as soon as he has it—"

"There's no other way, Joe," said Anna. She looked at him and moved her head down, almost imperceptibly. A nod. Keep arguing.

"I'd rather die than give anything to these fucks," said Joe. "I thought you had changed. I thought you were on our side."

"Shut it," said Boggins, to him. "Where's the copy, Anna?"

Anna opened her mouth. "It's—"

Joe started moving toward her at a measured speed. He hoped this would work, hoped he had understood Anna's idea.

"Don't fucking move," said Hawkins, raising his rifle. Joe froze. Anna moved closer to Boggins, backing away from Joe. Her hand grazed a desk, and she held something in her palm. Joe raised his hands.

"Dr. Marshall is merely smartening up, Mr. Amery," said Boggins. "Doctor. Where's the copy of our research?"

Everything happened quickly.

Anna slid behind Boggins, wrapping an arm around his throat, holding the syringe she had palmed up to his neck, sliding it in. Boggins yelled out in pain. Hawkins immediately pivoted, aiming his rifle at her. The rest of the soldiers turned to aim at her as well.

"Anyone moves, and Boggins gets air injected into him," said Anna. "Don't test me."

"Lower your weapons," said Boggins, to Hawkins and the mercs. Hawkins slowly lowered his rifle, as did the others. "Dr. Marshall, please, let's talk about this."

"Shut your mouth," said Anna. "We're going to get out of here—"

And then Gary and Sean charged the mercs. They had been quiet, and Joe had read it as fear. But they had been waiting, and Joe didn't stand on ceremony. Gunfire filled the room, but Joe didn't look, sprinting toward the steel door. Behind it were three dozen undead.

RATATAT

RATATAT

RATATAT

Burst gunfire filled the area, but Joe ignored it, and

jumped over the last desk, and pulled the door open.

The zombies were on the other side of the door, attracted by the noise, and now even more by the gunfire.

They poured into the room.

25

The zombies streamed into the room, and Joe dove behind a desk as the bullets flew, tucking himself underneath, hiding from both the mercs and the undead.

He ducked his head out, and saw Anna in the corner of the room, still holding Boggins close to her, the syringe in his neck. Hawkins had turned his attention to the dead, and was firing bursts of gunfire at them. The rifle was powerful, and would have torn apart a living target in seconds.

The creatures took the shots and kept coming. The rest of the mercs had been fighting off Sean and Gary. Gary laid still on the ground, blood pooling around him, gunned down by the mercs when they charged them. Sean was on top of one of them, struggling, trying to take their weapon, but then another pushed him away and fired point blank, and Sean fell, dead.

The bullets did nothing to the zombies, and they pushed through the tables and desks, battering anything that got in their way, rushing to the sound of the gunfire. The mercs opened fire, all blasting away at the dead as they approached.

Anna took the chance and pulled Boggins with her, past the mercs, pulling him out the door, getting away from the creatures. She didn't see him, and Joe didn't blame her for running. He was on his own.

Gunfire filled the area, and each shot reverberated in the room, Joe's body shaking with each blast. The zombies were being filled with lead, the soldiers targeting anything they could hit. But they kept coming. The soldiers were outnumbered and were trained to fight humans that went down when you hit center mass.

"Shoot 'em in the head!" yelled one merc.

"It's not doing anything!"

"What the fuck, what the fuck—"

And then a scream, as the zombies, filled with anger, pulled one down. He screamed, and screamed, and they dug into him with their fingers, pulling him apart with all the strength they had left.

"Stop them, stop them—"

More gunfire, as the rest of the mercs tried to save their brothers, but the bullets did nothing. The gunfire only attracted more of them, made them angrier, filled with more and more rage. They still came in through the holding area, and they crashed against the thin line of the mercs, who fired as long as they could, the rounds doing nothing, and then running out of room to even raise their rifles.

They screamed, screamed as the creatures overwhelmed

them.

Joe had to get out of there. If he ran, while the undead focused on the mercs, he could get through the door, and shut
and lock it behind him, and get out of here with Anna—

Then the desk that sheltered him was yanked away and
thrown to the side. Shit, the zombies had found him—

But it wasn't the dead. It was Hawkins. Joe had lost sight
of him, thought him dead along with his squad mates. Hawkins looked worse for wear, his armor torn, his face bloody,
his helmet gone. But he still stood. He had learned, and
stopped firing at the creatures, instead using his rifle as a
club, and beat them as they approached. There were a half
dozen of the zombies on the ground behind him, crawling
with outstretched hands. Hawkins had broken their legs
and kneecaps, crippling them.

"This is your fault," he said. "You motherfucker—" But
Hawkins wouldn't shoot Joe, to risk the ire of the undead,
and instead jumped on top of him, pressing the edge of his
rifle into Joe's neck. Joe put his hands out, pushing as hard
as he could, but Hawkins was bigger and stronger. He could
barely breathe.

"If I'm going, I'm taking you with me," said Hawkins, his
breath hot in Joe's face. "This was supposed to be routine—"

Joe struggled. He had little air left, and he saw spots in
his vision.

"That's right," said Hawkins. "Nighty night."

Joe thought of his mother. He thought of Helen. And he
thought of Nile, and his anger sparked an idea, a dying idea
in his oxygen deprived brain. It was his only chance.

He took one hand off the rifle as Hawkins pressed it hard
against his throat and slid it over to the trigger.

"What are you—" started Hawkins, and then Joe pulled, and the rifle fired a quick burst of bullets into the wall. The sound was cacophonous, so close to Joe's ear. But it was all he had.

"You think that'll do anythin—" and then the zombies came to the sound. All the other mercs were dead, ripped apart by the rage filled creatures, and now they had a new target, rushing over to the two of them. "No, no—" and then the undead were there, and Hawkins let go of Joe, turning to fight them off, but as he did, Joe held onto the rifle, and pulled. Hawkins lost his grip on the gun. Joe held it, and Hawkins had no weapon at all to defend himself.

The zombies piled on top of him, and he grunted, trying his best to fight them off. Joe scrambled to his feet, his breath coming hard, and he ran for the door. The creatures were thick in the room, but he shoved through them as they ripped at the mercs and at Hawkins, forcing his way past groping and pulling hands, the stinking undead trying to pull him down.

Joe ran, and the door was there, and he pushed through it and pulled it shut behind him, a hand getting caught in the door, and Joe slammed it harder, and a row of fingers fell to the floor. The door locked shut, and Hawkins screamed from behind it. The scream was soon cut short.

Joe turned, and Anna stood there, Boggins still clutched in front of her. She hadn't removed the syringe from his neck. Joe raised the rifle and pulled it to his shoulder, aiming at Boggins.

"You can let him go, Anna," said Joe, forcing his voice to stay calm. Anna pulled the syringe out in a smooth motion and threw it aside. Boggins grunted and clutched his neck, a thin stream of blood leaking out. Anna joined Joe.

Boggins stared at him with anger and fear.

"You—"

"No," said Joe, taking a single step forward with the rifle. "You don't talk anymore. You only answer questions. Or I'll shoot you." Boggins stared, his nostrils flaring, but said nothing.

"Tell us everything," said Joe. "Nile's plans."

Boggins stared at him with that same plain face. "I told you, Mr. Amery."

"Where are the employees?" asked Joe. "They should have come in by now."

"We got in contact with everyone important. We told them to get out of the city immediately. They've all evacuated. Everyone else was told to stay home."

"You didn't warn them?"

"We couldn't," said Boggins. "We couldn't let anyone know—"

"That you created this shit, yeah, I know," said Joe. "So you were telling the truth."

"Why would I lie?" asked Boggins.

"A lot of reasons," said Joe.

"I didn't," said Boggins. "Our eyes in the sky are already seeing signs of effect."

"You mean you've spotted fucking zombies in town, you piece of shit," said Joe. He walked up and put the barrel against his chest, and tapped him hard. "They're people. They have lives. Loved ones. Dreams, and hopes."

Boggins said nothing, and Joe tapped him again and he grimaced, but said nothing, and Joe felt the rage boil up him inside of him, the last few hours finally venting. He slammed the butt of the rifle across Boggins' chin and he went down in a heap, grunting.

"Nothing to say?" asked Joe. "Was your paycheck worth it, huh? Was your paycheck worth it?" Joe jammed the butt into Boggins' temple with a dull thud and Boggins fell, his eyes foggy.

"You're going to kill him," said Anna. Joe paused, holding the gun aloft.

"He deserves worse," said Joe. He looked down at Boggins, who bled now from his face, leaking from his forehead, where Joe had split him open. "Is there a cure?"

"A cure?" asked Boggins. "What exactly would that be?"

"I don't know—"

"The chemical kills them, Mr. Amery. The side effect is that it brings them back. There is no cure for death. Not yet, at least."

Joe raised the rifle. "Tell me why I shouldn't kill you right now."

"Is it true you have a copy of the research?" asked Boggins.

"Yes," said Joe. "On a thumb drive. I swallowed it before we were captured."

Boggins allowed himself a smile, slim and sinister. "We'll pay you for it."

"Bullshit," said Joe. "You'll kill me and take it."

"It's too late for that," said Boggins. "Clearly. But it's your last chance to escape this, Mr. Amery. For you and Dr. Marshall both."

"What are you talking about?" asked Joe. "We're out of here. You can't stop us."

Boggins stared at him, his smile vanishing. He sighed

and then chuckled. "Do you think the military would let this be? Do you think they'd let the undead roam freely? No. Of course not."

Boggins pushed himself off the floor, back to his feet. "The military is surrounding the town. Probably already have. Roadblocks set up at every road and highway. No one is getting out of the city."

"You're lying," said Anna.

"No, I'm not," said Boggins. "Again, why would I? Nile informed the military, and together they came up with a solution, one that will benefit them both in the long run." He looked again at Joe. "And it could benefit you. Give us back the research and you'll be a wealthy man. Both of you. Never have to worry about money for the rest of your life. Why shouldn't you kill me? Because keeping me alive will keep you alive. It'll get you out of this town and make sure you live the rest of your life in comfort."

"So, that's the deal?" asked Joe. "Keep you alive, turn over the copy of the research, and we live? Get paid a lot?"

"Yes," said Boggins. "More than you'll ever need."

Joe stared at Boggins' cold, inscrutable face. The face meant to be forgotten.

He thought of Wally.

Joe raised the rifle to his shoulder and shot Boggins in the head. The gunshot reverberated in the hallway, and the bullet hit Boggins in the eye, his brains splattering through the exit wound. He fell over, dead.

"I'd rather die."

26

It was afternoon by the time Joe and Anna saw daylight again.

Joe felt like he'd been inside for infinity, but it had been no longer than one of his extended shifts working in the fulfillment center. He hadn't known what they'd find when they emerged from the facility. Would it be chaos? Would there be smoke rising in the distance? Would there be zombies prowling in the parking lot, ready to charge, a sudden, unyielding rage seizing them at the sight of something living?

What they found was nothing.

Well, not nothing, but close to it.

"I've never seen the parking lot so empty," said Anna. The lots surrounding the Nile facility always were at least half full, with different shifts filing in and out of the fulfill-ment center as some worked through the night to make sure every package ordered at any hour would move through their system quickly.

But only a sparse few vehicles were parked in the mam-moth space. They saw Anna's SUV. A few other vehicles were spread out. One other massive vehicle caught their at-tention. It was right outside the facility, parked half on the curb.

It was an enormous black humvee, unmarked, but clear-ly was the vehicle used by the mercs. Joe carried the assault rifle he had taken from Hawkins, but he had no extra ammo, all of it in the room with the zombies, on what remained of the soldier's corpses.

"We need ammo," said Joe. "And you need a gun."

"Why?" asked Anna. "The zombies—they can't be killed."

"I'm not only worried about the undead," said Joe. "There's going to be people out there. And they're going to be just as dangerous."

"How are we going to get inside?" asked Anna. "The keys are probably on someone's corpse."

Joe tried the side door, and it opened, sliding open, re-vealing a huge inner area filled with equipment and seats. "I was going to suggest we break the window—" Joe found the clips for the assault rifle and an ammo bag to hold them. He slung it over one shoulder, with the heavy clips hung on his hip. He hoped he wouldn't need them.

Anna grabbed a pistol and some ammo of her own, tucking them into her back pockets. She strapped a holster around her waist. She fumbled with it for a few minutes, but finally got it situated.

"Have you fired a gun before?" asked Joe.

"Only when I was a kid," said Anna. "But like you said, it's not that complicated."

There was a moment of silence between them, and Joe listened to the air. He listened for the sound of sirens, or gunshots, or shouts.

But there was nothing. Springfield was dead.

They were armed, now.

Joe's phone vibrated in his pocket from an onslaught of notifications, suddenly getting service against after being in the black hole that was the Nile facility. The concrete blocked the cell signal. They had found their belongings in Nile's holding area, including his phone.

Joe scanned through them all. Nothing from his mom or Helen. He had to warn them, had to try.

He called his mom first, on her cell phone.

It rang through to voicemail. He tried a second time, but it rang through again. He tried the nursing home's phone. Maybe they would pick up. Surely, someone was there, someone had to be—

No answer.

Helen was next.

The same. No answer.

"Well?" asked Anna.

"No answer, anywhere," said Joe. "My mom, Helen. Nothing." Anna held his stare for a second and then looked away. She opened her own phone.

"Nothing on the news," said Anna. "There's no updates on Channel 9's website since yesterday."

"Or Channel 6," said Joe. "I know. I can try the local radio station." He opened the app on his phone and booted up the signal. He turned his volume up all the way.

Nothing. Only a thin crackle, once in a while.

"Dead air," said Anna.

"Don't radio stations run themselves?" asked Joe. "Shouldn't there at least be some music playing?"

"Someone still has to push the buttons," said Anna. "No one's there."

"There has to be someone, somewhere," said Joe. "The whole town can't have been affected yet."

"How would anyone know?" asked Anna. "We can't worry about it. We'll find survivors as we go."

"Go where?" asked Joe. "I need to get to my mom. I need to check on Helen. And Betsy."

Anna looked at him, and then looked away, and then back. "We need to upload the files. If the military is out there—they may cut the internet, take out cell phone towers. Who knows? They probably don't know we got out of there yet. We have to take advantage."

Joe looked away. His heart screamed to go get his mom. To save her. To help Helen. To do something.

But they had done all this to stop Nile. To show them they were vulnerable. That they couldn't get away with their plans. And it had only gotten worse in the meantime, and Nile's plan was only bigger. If they didn't get the word out— Nile would win.

And that was bigger than him, and bigger than his mom, and Helen, and anything. He couldn't stomach it.

"All we have is each other," said Joe, finally, under his breath.

"What'd you say?"

"You're right," said Joe. "Let's go. Do you have a plan?"

"Do you have a PC at Helen's?"

"No," said Joe. "Only my phone."

"I have a desktop. The internet will hopefully still work. We can upload the files there. I'll send them to every reporter with a pulse. They won't be able to stop all of them."

"Think we can still drive?"

"I don't know," said Anna. "I sure as hell hope so, though. It's a twenty-minute drive, and six-hour walk."

"Maybe we can find a motorcycle," said Joe. "Should be easier to navigate with."

"Can you drive one?"

"Well enough," said Joe. "Even a bike would be faster than on a foot. We can sure as hell find those if we need to. After we upload the files—will you—will you help me? Help me with my mom?"

Anna met his eyes. "Yes, of course," she said. Anna raised the key fob and hit the button. A distant beep rung through the air. Her car was still there.

"We can take my car," said Anna. "My apartment. Then Helen and your mom. Alright?"

"Yeah," said Joe. "Maybe Boggins was lying, and it won't be so bad. Maybe it's only—"

A distant revving noise suddenly came within earshot.

"You hear that?" asked Anna.

"What the hell—"

It got louder and louder. It was an engine. Coming closer.

"It wouldn't be the military, would it?" asked Joe. He raised his rifle. "They couldn't know, not this soon—"

The engine got louder, and then the source turned the corner on the adjacent street, coming into view. It was a pickup truck, a big one. Solid white. Well, it had been, but there were dings and dents all over it, including a massive crumple in the front right corner. As it got closer, Joe saw the paint was stained red.

"What the hell—" said Anna, and the truck kept moving, the accelerator pushed to the floor, the engine screaming. It was coming toward them.

"Go, run!" yelled Joe, and he ran back toward the building. There were traffic blockers in front of the doors. They were only a few hundred feet away. He sprinted, and Anna ran with him. He heard the engine roar behind him, and the truck gained ground on them, even as it hopped curbs and ran through signs.

The driver had seen them, and was aimed right at them. The engine roared, and Joe didn't look back, only running. It was on top of him. They had escaped the facility, just to die to this, all of this for nothing—

And then they both reached the row of concrete safety dividers, and rushed through them, and kept running, god knows what would happen—

A calamitous noise followed them, the sound of crunching and tearing metal, followed by nothing.

Joe turned and looked. The truck had smashed into the concrete barriers, and they had withstood the impact.

The truck was destroyed, the hood and engine compartment smashed, and oil leaked out onto the ground below. The vehicle would never drive again.

"What the fuck is happening?" asked Anna.

"I don't think we're going to ask the driver," said Joe. "There's no way they would have survived—"

And then the door cracked open, or as much as it could, the frame of the truck bent and shifted. A body fell out, groaning, muttering.

"There's no way," said Anna. "It was going a hundred miles an hour."

"He's not alive," said Joe, staring at the zombie as it crawled to its feet. Its face was a shattered wreck, blood and bone making it unrecognizable. Two white orbs peered out from the bloody mess and turned to look at them.

"It's impossible," said Anna. The creature moaned again and turned toward them, moving as fast as it could on its crippled legs, dragging one behind it. It wanted them. It wanted to destroy them.

Joe raised the assault rifle to his shoulder and fired, aiming at the creature's legs. He shot three bursts, and the rifle kicked hard into his shoulder. The first burst missed entirely, but the second and third both landed in the legs of the creature, and it fell, and could no longer stand.

"Hawkins had the right idea," said Joe. "Take out their legs, and they can only crawl after you."

The zombie still tried to get them, pulling itself along with its arms, scratching at the pavement. It moaned.

"What is it saying?" asked Anna. The creature repeated the same phrase, over and over again.

"I can't tell," said Joe. They approached the creature, staying just out of reach as it clawed toward them. "I think its jaw is broken." The zombie had once been a man, dressed in business attire.

"Sell, se—sell," muttered the thing, as it tried to attack, even with its mangled and shattered limbs.

"Sell," said Joe.

"Sell what?"

"Who knows?" asked Joe. "Could have been anything."

"They can still drive."

"They retain some information," said Joe. "Whatever was drilled into their brain." Joe stared at the creature's broken face. "All he remembers is work."

27

If he didn't look too closely, Joe didn't notice a difference once they pulled onto the highway. Sure, the roads were mostly empty, but there was never that much traffic on this side of town, especially during off hours. The lights were still running. They occasionally passed another vehicle.

Sure, some drove a little erratically. But that also wasn't that much different from normal. There were always bad drivers.

At first, at least. But then the amount of crashed or stalled cars became too many to ignore.

Or the stray people wandering near the highway. Or on the highway.

Of course, they weren't people anymore. They had died, and then come back.

Anna drove, with Joe riding shotgun. He kept his rifle ready, just in case. None of the zombies had approached the car yet, and all the traffic they had encountered was going the other way. Joe didn't know what they knew, or what their plans were, but he was happy for them to stay out of his way. Maybe in the ensuing days, they would want help. But for now, any other people were dangerous. Alive or dead.

"How far?" asked Joe.

"Not very," said Anna. "Another five minutes. At least the roads have been clear. If they were shut down—" Anna trailed off.

They'd be in a shit ton of trouble. Joe finished the thought in his head. They passed an ambulance on its side, the lights still flashing. The back was open, the contents spilling out onto the highway.

"I think we can forget the idea that it isn't widespread," said Anna.

"Probably a safe bet," said Joe. He pushed the thoughts of his mom, of Helen, of Betsy even, out of his head. They would get to them in time. Spreading the word was more important, and there was safety in numbers. Anna couldn't do it without him, not with the thumb drive still inside him. They had to get word out about Nile. It would be erased without them, and worse still, be used again. They had to salt the earth about the idea. If it became accepted, if it became commonplace—there would be no stopping it.

Anna slammed on the brakes, and Joe grabbed onto the handle of the door.

"What the hell—"

"There's a man in the road," said Anna. "A living one."

Just from his movement alone, it was clear he wasn't a

zombie. As they pulled closer, his injuries were plain to see. His clothes were ripped, and blood stained them. He was limping.

Then the source of his wounds became clear.

A horde of the creatures were chasing him. They ran with loping gaits, some faster than others, but they followed him. Joe pictured it in his mind, at first one following, and then another joining, and another, and another. All seeing a target, like a greyhound with a rabbit. No thought beyond something to destroy, a primordial urge, uncontrollable now, without the burden of consciousness, without any rational thought holding it back. The base hunter instinct was now in control.

"Help!" yelled the man, waving at them. He saw them, his eyes wide. "Please, help!"

"Don't stop," said Joe, quickly. Anna had slowed down, a hundred feet away from the man and the horde of zombies. The man himself had slowed to wave at them. The horde was close.

"He'll die," said Anna.

"He might die even if we stop," said Joe. "The thumb drive is more important. Like you said. Keep going. We can't save everyone."

Anna looked over at him for a long moment, her eyes reading him, and then swerved around the man and the zombies, crossing over several lanes of traffic, accelerating away. The man yelled again, but his voice was soon gone, and he was gone, out of sight. Silence filled the vehicle.

"I know it's hard," said Joe. "But we have to—we have to take care of ourselves."

Anna drove, and soon she pulled off the highway, onto

a surface road.

"My complex is right up here. It's gated, so maybe it won't—" and then they saw it, the complex on the left, called Carlton Arms, a new sign with fancy lettering, green and stark white. A gated complex, everything new. Joe bet it was expensive to live there.

It didn't protect them. The gate had been destroyed, the metal pushed back off the track, dented and broken, pushed out of the way. A thin stream of smoke drifted up from the engine block of the car embedded in the gate. The hood was crumpled, and the driver's side door was open. Anna crept forward, just enough room for her vehicle to get through. She gasped softly, looking over at the car.

A body laid next to it, face down. It was an older woman with white hair.

"I—I knew her," said Anna. "Her name was Beatrice. She would feed the ducks by the pond."

Anna continued on. Joe kept his head on a swivel, his eyes scanning every doorway they passed, every bush. They could come from any direction. Aside from the carnage at the entrance, the rest of the complex looked relatively normal. Cars in the parking lot. No more corpses.

Joe had his rifle ready. Anna pulled into a parking spot.

They got out, and Joe listened for anything. Mutterings from a zombie, or cries for help, or gunshots. But there was nothing, not right now. Good. They could get in and out.

They got out of the car, and Joe followed Anna as they hustled to her apartment. He kept the rifle up and tight to his shoulder, the ammo bag slung around him. If anything came at them, he would be ready.

But nothing did. Joe looked at each of her neighbor's

doors as they passed, but none of them moved, and there was no sound. The climb was quick and uneventful, and they were at her door, and then through. Anna unlocked it, and they slipped inside, locking the door behind them.

Joe felt like he could breathe again, just having that measure of peace and security, having a locked door between him and whatever the hell was out there. He leaned back against the wall and let the rifle hang. He realized his jaw had been clenched tight, and he relaxed it.

"Joe," said Anna.

"Sorry," he said. "I just needed to breathe for a second." Anna's apartment seemed relatively normal, a small one-bedroom unit, with a kitchen and living room. It was sparsely decorated, with some bland framed art that looked to be from Target.

"Well, the power is still on," said Anna. "Remember, don't use the water."

"Can we touch it?" asked Joe. "I would think it's only if it gets inside you."

"I don't know," said Anna. "It's best not to risk it."

"Well, easy for you to say," said Joe. "I still have a thumb drive inside me. And we need it if we're going to upload those files."

"Use the guest bathroom," said Anna. "Do what you have to. I'll get on my PC and see if the internet is still working. Gather the contacts, so we can send it out."

Joe nodded. "Do you have any bottled water?"

"I just bought a case," said Anna. "It's in the pantry."

"Good. We'll need it."

*

Joe emerged from the bathroom twenty minutes later with the thumb drive.

He found Anna in her bedroom, at her desk in the corner. She had two monitors up, and was typing things into a spreadsheet.

"Internet working?"

"For now," said Anna. "Still no real news out about Springfield. Some stuff floating around online, but none of it has been picked up by any news orgs. Not yet, at least. As people try and get into the area, and find blockades and roadblocks, word will spread quickly. How'd it go?"

He held out the thumb drive. "It wasn't pretty, but it's here."

"Let's hope it still works," said Anna. "Plug it in."

Joe popped off the cap and slotted it into the front USB of her tower. Anna opened the drive.

"It's all there," said Anna, letting out a deep breath. Joe felt his heart beat hard, and a rush of emotion filled him. He fought back tears. It wasn't for nothing.

"Who are you sending it to?"

"I have a list," said Anna. "I've been compiling it over the last couple weeks. Looking for labor journalists, investigative journalists, people who've covered Nile in the past, plus some more well-known figures. I'll be sending them the files directly, as well as uploading them to a dozen cloud services. We don't really care who breaks the story, as long as the information is out there. I've been writing our experiences for the past couple weeks as well, and I'll be adding that, as well as what happened last night, and what is happening to Springfield. Do you want to look it over before I send it?"

"I trust you," said Joe. "Send it."

Anna clicked once, and then twice, attaching the info, uploading it where it needed to go. After a couple minutes, she clicked send, and the messages sent.

"It's through," she said. She exhaled. "It'll be everywhere soon. It's out of our control, at least for the moment."

Joe stared at the computer. It felt unreal, everything he had done to try to hurt Nile, and it had worked. The files would be seen by the entire world soon enough.

It's your fault. The town is dying, and it's your fault.

That wasn't fair. He hadn't known, had only done what he thought was best. Nile deserved to be destroyed, deserved to be stopped. It was worth—

What about Helen? What about Mom?

Joe silenced the voice inside. They might still be okay. He pushed burning guilt inside away, down deeper, and forgot about it. He did the right thing, and now they would go get Helen and Mom, and they would find a way out of Springfield. Nile knew what he did, and did nothing to warn anyone. It was their fault, it was their fault, none of this would have happened if they hadn't done such horrible things to begin with—

"Let me grab a few things and we can go," said Anna. "We should pack up all the bottled water, all the canned foods. Anything we can carry."

"I'll work on it," said Joe.

They packed up what they could.

"I'll start loading up," said Joe. He carried the case of bottled water in his hands, his rifle slung around his back, and he opened the door, and went outside, and then he heard the muttering, a chittering noise coming from his right, and *fuck* he had already gotten careless, just from an hour being safe, and the zombie was on top of him and the bottled water fell from his hands as he put them up, trying to fend off the thing.

It had been a woman, young, but now her eyes were lifeless, filled only with murderous rage, and Joe grabbed her wrists, which were reaching for his eyes.

Please no

He struggled with her, and he realized how tired he was, how much little was left in his tank, with this thing giving all it could to hurt him, and soon it would push him down, and he couldn't stop it, and he tried to yell for Anna but he didn't have the breath, and she was inside the apartment—

"Anna!" he forced out, and he hoped she heard it, but he couldn't hold off this creature for much longer, and he couldn't reach for his gun, god, not like this, he had to save his mom—

The zombie pushed, and it would be on top of him, here on the landing, and Anna would come out to this monster ripping out his throat, and then he saw the stairs.

Fuck me

The zombie pushed him over, but he pulled it sideways, and they tumbled down the stairs, and Joe tucked his head, hoping he wouldn't die. They fell hard, two sacks of potatoes banging off the stone steps and metal railing. They rolled down a flight, hit the end hard and a huge CRACK rang out.

Joe still held onto the zombie's wrists, and thought for a second his neck was broken, and this was how he would die, but then his legs kicked in and he pushed himself up, and let go of the creature, and scrambled up the stairs.

It wasn't his neck that was broken, but hers. The creature's head was cocked at an awful, impossible angle, and the bones jutted against the skin terribly. It still struggled to move, trying to force its broken body to come after him.

Joe watched it struggle, breathing hard, his hands on his knees. Anna emerged from the apartment behind him, after hearing him yell.

"What happened?" asked Anna. She looked down and saw the zombie. "Oh, fuck. Are you okay?"

"Yeah, I'm fine," said Joe. "Was careless for a second. She almost got me. You know her?"

"Well, I did," said Anna. "Her name was Cheryl."

28

They loaded up Anna's SUV with all the bottles of water, plus all the canned food she had, piled into canvas grocery bags. The body of Anna's former neighbor still floundered at the bottom of the steps, trying its best to move, but it couldn't, its spine snapped.

Helen's apartment wasn't far, not on the highway, only a ten-minute drive.

But that was with a functioning traffic system. The highway had been mostly clear on the way to Anna's, but that stretch was far from the center of the city. As they got closer to the city center and to Helen's apartment, the highway was at a standstill.

They looked ahead at a field of stopped cars, across all the lanes. People wandered around the traffic.

"Hard to say if they're alive or dead," said Joe.

"Might be both," said Anna.

"We can't go this way," said Joe. "We'll have to drive through neighborhoods. We can get there through surface streets. It'll just take longer."

"Won't it be dangerous?" asked Anna. "Even if people haven't turned—they'll be defending their homes—"

"Whatever it is, it's the only way that isn't on foot. We can't drive through whatever the hell this is."

Anna looked at him and shrugged. "Alright." She turned a quick U-turn and then right down a surface street, into a neighborhood. The GPS was still working, and they told it to avoid highways. But there was no way for them to tell it to avoid the creatures, or the surface streets that were blocked.

They turned down street after street, getting incrementally closer to Helen's apartment complex. But after just a few streets, it became clear that the chaos was not confined to the blocked highway.

They had thought that because the roads near Nile were clear, that the rest of the roads would stay empty as well. But Joe now realized the reason the road was clear was because, well, there just weren't that many people that lived out there. Housing wasn't very dense.

Inside the city, there were decades of homes and apartments, all right next to each other. All filled with people, with families. And now, those people were one of two things: undead, or fighting them off.

Crashed cars, wandering zombies, fleeing people. There were no quiet streets in Springfield, not anymore.

People ran by, screaming for help. Anna didn't slow down. They couldn't afford to, not here. This wasn't a lone case of a person sprinting from a handful of zombies. A person would run by every other minute, screaming for help, or more often, not yelling at all. They were only worried about running.

The undead were in greater number. They had swarmed, over a dozen of the creatures chasing someone together.

Cars were stranded in the streets, ran into street signs or concrete mailboxes, or simply abandoned, the driver dying, turning undead, and leaving the car in the middle of the road.

"Hop the curb!" yelled Joe, as a swarm of zombies turned toward them, as they drove down one street.

Anna jerked the wheel to the right and the car thumped as they drove up onto the sidewalk, and then through someone's yard, tearing up the grass. The swarm followed Anna, but she sped up, hopping back onto the road and driving, swerving around another errant zombie whose attention they'd drawn. She could have run it down, but it was just another risk. They couldn't lose the vehicle, not now. They'd be stranded.

"Jesus Christ," said Anna, under her breath. "Only five minutes."

"If the rest of the path is clear," said Joe.

They came to the end of the street, and they turned again, and the street was clear, and they could ride this all the way to the apartment complex. Anna went, speeding up cautiously. There didn't seem to be anything more in their way, they'd finally get off the road, even for a second. They'd find Helen, and Betsy, and get them out of here, and out to the nursing home. Once they had his mom, they could find a way out of the city, there had to be a gap, somewhere—

"What the hell—" muttered Anna, and Joe looked. There were zombies ahead, dozens of them, but they were all on the ground, all floundering, all crawling—

Then a gunshot cracked, and they both jumped, and a lone standing zombie fell.

"Someone's picking them off," said Joe. "They figured out to take out their legs."

"I can't go through—"

"Drive over them," said Joe.

"Joe, I don't know—"

"You have to," said Joe. "Just keep going, the car should make it."

Anna opened her mouth to speak, but instead said nothing, taking a deep breath, closing and opening her eyes, and driving forward, and then the wheels went over the first bump, the first zombie, bones and organs crushed underneath the wheels of the heavy car, and the SUV slowed, and Anna pushed hard on the accelerator, and the car bumped up and down as they drove over the bodies of the undead, wriggling underneath them.

BANG BANG BANG

"What the fuck?" asked Joe, and then more shots rang out—

"They're firing at us!" yelled Anna, and she floored it, driving over more bodies.

"We're not zombies, fuckhead!" yelled Joe, although there was no way they heard, it didn't matter, and more shots rang out, and bullets hit the car with a THUNK, and he ducked his head.

"Fuck, drive, drive!" yelled Joe, and Anna floored it, and they finally were over the speedbump zombies and they drove away. A couple more gunshots rang out, but they didn't hit the SUV, and they were gone.

"Jesus fuck," said Joe, his heart pounding in his chest. "You okay? Is the car okay?"

"I'm fine," said Anna. "Car seems fine. Everything's still working."

"If we turn right at the end of this street, the backside of the complex will be on our left," said Joe. Anna turned, and Joe saw the familiar sight. It had been less than a day since he left Helen's place, to destroy Nile's operation and reveal the truth to the world. It felt like years had passed.

"There's a gate here, but it's almost always locked—"

The gate *was* locked, but Anna turned and floored the SUV, and the lock snapped immediately, not able to withstand the force.

"We're not going around," said Anna. "Where's her place?"

"Right here on the left," said Joe. The parking lot seemed normal, mostly empty during the middle of the day. Anna pulled into a spot, and they surveyed the area, looking for any stray zombies, or people. After whoever shot at them, everyone was a threat.

"Nothing in sight," said Joe. "I say if there's only one or two of the zombies, we do our best to avoid them. Gunfire will only attract more."

"If there's more than one or two?"

"Then we do what we have to."

Anna nodded, and they got out, and Joe moved quickly to Helen's apartment. He grabbed a backpack he had taken from Anna's. He had filled it with water bottles. Joe glanced over the parking lot, looking, and then he saw it. Helen's car, an old Subaru. She hadn't left this morning. He didn't know if that was good or not.

Joe heard mutterings, and saw a figure move slowly on the other side of the complex's courtyard, but he kept moving. If it wasn't an immediate threat, he wouldn't fire. The noise would attract them, and they would group, and that's when they became dangerous.

He gestured toward Helen's door, and pulled out his key, and slid it into the lock. It caught the deadbolt, meaning it was still locked. The lock clicked open, and Joe eased the door open, pushing in, and then suddenly there was movement, and something smashed into his leg, and he panicked—

And then he realized it was Betsy. He pushed in, petting her, and Anna shut the door behind them. The hallway light was the only light inside, but it was enough to see by.

"Hey girl," said Joe, grabbing Betsy, hugging her, as her tail wagged at warp speed. Anna reached down to pet her, and Betsy treated her like an old friend. "Well, Betsy made it. Her kibble is in a bin in the kitchen. Will you feed her and get her some bottled water? I'm going to find Helen."

Anna nodded, and found Betsy's water bowl, filling it with a bottle. Betsy greedily lapped at it. She was thirsty.

"Helen," called Joe. He didn't want to yell too loudly. There was no answer. The apartment wasn't big. If she was in here, she would hear him. The kitchen was empty, with only Betsy and Anna in it. Joe went to the living room next, also empty, still filled with Joe's stuff. The guest bathroom door was open, the interior dark.

"Helen," he called again, a little louder. Still nothing. He slowed. All that was left was her bedroom. The light was on, reflecting out into the hallway, and he called one more time. "Helen."

There was no answer from inside, and he cautiously pushed the door open, peeking his head in.

Nothing.

Where the hell could she be?

Her car was still here. Had she gone out on foot? Had she caught a ride with someone else to get out? She didn't carpool to work, as far as Joe knew. She had to be somewhere, but it wasn't here. Helen hadn't answered her phone. He would try her again in a little while, and maybe she'd answer, and he would at least know if she—

And there was a clattering noise, and Joe realized.

Her bathroom.

"Helen?" he asked, walking into her bedroom, toward her bathroom door, which was tucked in the near corner. The door was closed, but a thin sliver of light shone from underneath. She didn't answer.

He raised a fist to the door, slightly shaking, and knocked once, twice. If she was inside, there was no ignoring it.

There was no answer, for a moment, and Joe's hand closed on the handle, and then there was something.

"Ungg—connection—two—two, two," came from behind the door, a drone, but one Joe recognized as from Helen. More muttered words reached him, none of them making sense, and his heart dropped, and a deep cold spike filled his guts, and his hand squeezed hard on the handle, and tears welled in the corners of his eyes.

"She's gone, Joe," said Anna, from behind him. She had come in, quiet. "Whatever's in there, it's not her anymore."

Joe squeezed his eyes shut and forced the tears back. If

he let them out now, there would be no end to it, no end to the onslaught, the crushing reality of what had happened to his town, what those chemicals had done, what *he* had done, all hitting at once. He couldn't let that out right now. It would kill him. They still needed to find his mom, and get out of town. There was no time for guilt or sadness. They had to survive.

He inhaled through his nose, forcing the tears away. He turned back toward Anna, who looked at him with sad eyes.

"I fed Betsy," said Anna.

"Good," said Joe.

"Joe, I—"

"Let's gather what we can from the pantry," said Joe. "And go find my mom."

29

The roads were getting worse by the second. Anna swerved back and forth, around zombies, around bodies, around abandoned cars, and around screaming survivors.

They couldn't stop, not yet. They had to get to the retirement home.

Anna's phone, which was positioned in the middle of the dash to help with GPS, suddenly lost service.

"Fuck," said Anna. "Towers are out."

"Why would the towers be out?" asked Joe. "If anything, there'd be less demand now, with so many people dead."

"Probably because the military has gotten wind of our leak. It's been enough time. Someone has spilled the beans, and the military doesn't want any more news coming out from Springfield. They want to control it. Don't know if they'll be able to. But they'll try. This is part of it. I'm assuming all internet is probably gone, too. Hope you can get me to the retirement home."

"I can guide you," said Joe. "At least get you in the general vicinity. It'll do well enough."

"Power's out, too," said Anna. "Traffic lights are all off."

"Not that it matters anymore," said Joe.

"It'll matter for frozen food," said Anna. "It'll last the day, maybe. Some of the grocery stores probably have backup generators. Might be our best bet, after we find your mom. Hole up in a Walmart, or a Costco."

"If no one else has beaten us to the punch," said Joe. Thoughts of Helen rose in his mind, of her trapped in that bathroom, until she rotted, until there was nothing left of her, until— "You'll want to turn north at some point."

"I'm looking for a chance," said Anna. The roads were a mess, and Anna couldn't stay on any one street for too long. They had hopped back onto the highway briefly, only to hop back off. Anna crossed medians freely now, not worrying about obeying any traffic laws. They hadn't seen any other moving vehicles since they'd left Helen's apartment.

Anna turned north, a swarm of zombies ahead on the road, all standing in a mass.

"You don't think it spreads, do you?" asked Anna, out of the blue.

"I don't know," said Joe. "It's from the chemical, right? That's what causes everything. Can the zombies put the chemical into the living, or the newly dead? If they can, maybe it can be spread."

"Because if it's only in the people who've drank the water, then we just have to wait it out. Eventually, they'll fall apart, and then there will be no more zombies."

"That might be awhile," said Joe. "Decomposition can take months."

"It's something, at least," said Anna. "Just trying to plan ahead. If we can't get out of the city, we'll have to survive at least as long as the undead do—" And then the wheel spun suddenly to the left.

"What's wrong?"

"I'm losing control," said Anna. "I don't know—" She pulled the wheel to the left, next to the curb.

"You can't stop here," said Joe. "We're right in the middle of a neighborhood. We'll get taken out—"

"It's not responding, Joe, I don't know what else to do," said Anna. "No gas, the wheel is sluggish—" And then the engine sputtered out and died.

"Fuck!" yelled Joe. Betsy whined from the back seat. Joe opened the door and looked under the car. A thin stream of oil was pouring from the engine block. "Fuck!" He yelled again. He looked to the side of the SUV and spotted the problem. One of the stray bullets from earlier had punched through the side of the car.

"One of the bullets took out an oil hose or something," said Joe. "We need to move. Your car is done."

"Fuck," said Anna. "What do we do?"

"Grab a bag and put only water in it," said Joe. "I'll do the same. I'll leave room for Betsy. I don't want her walking. We'll only lose her."

Joe jumped back out of the car and glanced around. The area was clear for now, but it was impossible to tell if it would stay that way. A horde of zombies could turn a corner at any moment, and they'd be overwhelmed.

Joe found a backpack and hastily pulled out food cans from it. Food had a much smaller chance of being contaminated. Their water supply would be finite until they purified the water from the taps. He ripped apart bottled water cases and dumped them into the backpack. It was a big backpack, one of Helen's camping bags, but still, it only had so much room. And he needed to leave room for Betsy inside. He hoped she would stay once he put her in.

"Behind you!" yelled Anna, and Joe turned to see a trio of zombies, all moving toward them. They muttered gibberish, and Joe turned and fired at their legs. He was becoming a better shot quickly, and with four bursts, the three zombies were on the ground, all now pulling themselves toward him, but doing so slowly. They'd be long gone by the time they reached them. But the gunfire would attract more.

He turned, threw a couple more bottles of water in, and then grabbed Betsy, who was standing on the seat, wagging her tail at him. She didn't know about the danger, and luckily wasn't spooked by the gunshots. Joe squeezed her butt into the backpack, and then zipped it up around her, leaving only her head and the top of her torso hanging out.

"I need you to stay in here, okay girl?" asked Joe. Betsy only stared back, but she didn't struggle, and Joe slung the backpack on. He hoped she would stay. "You ready?"

"Yeah, got everything I can carry in this backpack," she said. "And another tote full of bottled water."

"It'll have to do," said Joe. "We need to find another vehicle. We're sitting ducks on foot. It'll take us hours to get to the home walking." He looked up and down the street, and then back to the side street. "There's a Jeep down that way. Looks empty. We can take that, as long as it runs."

He started jogging, keeping his head on a swivel. He saw a horde of zombies a few hundred yards away. They hadn't noticed them yet. If they could get to the Jeep quickly, they'd be gone before the creatures even realized they were here. Anna was right behind him, and soon was ahead of him. Her cardio was better, and Joe soon was panting, trying to keep up. The Jeep was only a quarter mile away, but it felt like forever. The extra weight of the water and of Betsy was killing him. They needed a car. There was no way they'd make it to Mom without one.

As they drew closer, the Jeep looked empty, and there were no zombies around it, or bodies on the ground.

"Let's hope it runs," said Joe, through harried breath, and then Anna got to the car, and opened the driver's side door, and then she screamed, and Joe had only looked away for a second, and there was a zombie, pushing her over, the tote bag full of water falling onto the ground.

"Anna!" he yelled, running to her. The zombie had still been inside the Jeep, slumped over, and Anna hadn't seen it until it was too late. The thing was on her now, and she had her hands up, trying to keep the thing from killing her. Joe was right behind her, and then he was there, and my god, the zombie was huge, the man had to have weighed over three hundred pounds. He looked like a football player, or a bouncer, and shooting him would do no good. The creature muttered inarticulate rage on top of her, as Anna kept his hands off her.

"Help, help!" yelled Anna from underneath. He was crushing her, trying to rip her apart, and Anna could only hold him back for so long. Joe tried to push the fucker off, but he was too big. Joe wasn't strong enough, and he pushed and pushed.

"Move back," forced out Anna. Joe stepped back. What was she doing?

Anna shifted, and then suddenly she had her gun up underneath the zombie, and she fired, over and over and over, directly into his guts.

What are you doing, Anna, that won't do anything—

And it didn't, the gunfire absorbed by the creature, but it still struggled on top of her.

"Fuck," said Anna, her voice quiet. Joe grabbed the butt of his rifle and slid it between them. He'd use it as a goddamn lever to get it off her if he had to. He forced the gun between them, and slowly pushed the heavy thing off Anna.

The zombie then coughed violently, and a torrent of blood spewed from its mouth, all over Anna, and Joe pushed harder, throwing all of his weight behind it, and the creature fell to the ground, tumbling to the side. Joe raised his rifle and shot the thing in its legs, shattering the bones in its knees and shins. He pulled Anna away from the zombie, to give them some room to breathe, and then he looked at her—

Oh, no. Oh god no.

Her face was covered in the zombie's blood, a dark red crimson mask. But worse, it was in her eyes. She was blinking them, waving at them, and Joe grabbed for a bottle of water, and unscrewed it, handing it to her frantic hands and she poured it over her face, and into her eyes, and then he handed her another, and she did it again. She was covered in blood, and Joe ripped a piece of cloth off his shirt, tearing at it until it pulled away, and gave it to her as well, and she wiped her eyes clean.

She's got that shit in her now, Joe, there isn't any getting it out—

She looked at him, her eyes focusing on him. Anna could see. She was fine.

She was fine.

The creature struggled on the ground, but they could get around it. Joe grabbed the fallen tote bag and threw the water bottles that had tumbled out back inside.

"You okay?" he asked, going back to her. "Let's get going, the horde will be this way any second—"

"Joe—"

"God, that was close," he said. "Come on, Anna, we can take the Jeep, just have to step around that big fuck—"

"Joe, I can't go with you," said Anna, her voice quiet.

"What are you talking about?" he asked. He tried to hand her the tote bag. "I'll drive, if your eyes are bothering you—"

"Joe, stop. Look at me," she said. She sat on the ground. Anna was covered in the thing's blood. She had washed some of her face clean, but it still stained parts of it, and her chest and stomach were stained red. "It got in my eyes, Joe."

"Maybe it won't do anything," he said. "Maybe you'll be alright."

"I don't think so," said Anna. "I don't think so." She looked down, and held back something, and then looked back at him. "I can't go with you. It's too dangerous."

No no no no—

"Anna, I won't leave you," said Joe. "We won. We stopped them. You can't stop now."

"Joe, please," said Anna. "It's inside me. I don't know how long it takes, but it's not long. Leave me. Take Betsy. Find your mom. Find someplace safe. We got the word out." She stopped, and coughed. She swallowed something and shook her head.

"Anna, we can't leave you here. We don't know if it even spreads through their blood. You might be fine—"

Anna doubled over then, and coughed, and a thin gout of liquid poured from her mouth, and she coughed, and vomited some more. She coughed and spit, and then stood up and shook her head.

"Look at me, Joe," she said. "It's already—" and she coughed again, a horrible, hoarse noise. She swallowed. "It's—it's in me."

"Anna—"

She pulled up the pistol and pointed it at him. "I'm not asking, Joe. Take the water, and the Jeep, and get the fuck out of here."

No, this wasn't right—we won, we got out of there; we stopped them, this isn't how it goes—

"Anna—"

"Go!" she yelled. "Now."

Joe met her gaze, her eyes still stained with blood, and he nodded. "Okay. Okay." He turned, stopped, looked back. "I'm sorry, Anna."

"Not your fault," she said. "We did what we could. Go."

Joe went.

30

Joe stared down at his fingernails as he sat in the cancer ward's waiting area. They were chewed down, and ugly. He'd always bitten his nails, despite his many attempts to stop, but they were maybe the worst they'd ever been.

The anxiety always made it worse.

The waiting area was nice. Well-lit, air-conditioned, with comfortable seating, and quiet. Music played, but softly, softly enough some earbuds could tune it out. Plenty of magazines to read. Not that Joe ever read them.

Until recently, he'd tried to study while he waited for his mom. Read whatever book was up next in his class, or try to punch out some of a paper on his laptop.

But he couldn't focus, not here. His thoughts only went to his mom, the scrambling feeling in his guts too strong to formulate words, or to read, or to absorb any kind of information. After a while he stopped trying, walking miles around the hospital grounds instead, waiting for his mother's treatment to be over, a few hours of poison flowing through his mom every week. The walking kept his body busy, the only thing that allayed the anxiety. But, it didn't help getting his studying done.

Not that it mattered anymore.

He would return to the waiting area right before her time was up, and sit down, and wait for her to come out. She had walked into the first treatment strong, and able, but lately, she would hobble out, her bones aching, her hair gone, her skin sallow.

Another couple months of this, and then her first round of treatments would be over. Then they would wait, and let her recover, and then test to see if the cancer had gone into remission.

But that was too far away. Like his mom, Joe was taking it one day at a time.

A few minutes passed and his mom came out from the treatment area, her arm bandaged, not using a cane or walker even though she should. It had taken him a moment to recognize her, transformed in such a short amount of time.

"You need any help?" he asked.

"No, I'll be alright," she said. "It's not terrible until later." Still, he moved close to her, ready to catch her if she fell. They walked out, back to his car, and he stood by her as she got in, and waited until she was sitting, and only then climbed behind the wheel.

He turned the car over and headed back to the apartment.

"Thank you for driving me," she said. "You know, if you need to do something else, I could always get a taxi."

"No," said Joe. "Absolutely not. I'm not going to leave you to do this alone. It's hard enough as it is."

She stared out the windshield as Joe drove.

"You haven't been bringing your books," she said, her voice light as air.

"No," said Joe. He didn't want to talk about this right now.

"How are your classes going?"

Joe took a deep breath. He wouldn't lie to her. "I don't have any classes."

"What?"

"I dropped out, Mom."

"What do you mean, you dropped out?" she asked, her voice raising.

"Please, Mom, calm down."

"I will not," she said. "You worked hard to get into college, and now you've dropped out?"

"Mom—"

"You can't just throw away your future like that—"

"Mom, I'm not—"

"Don't Mom me, you need a degree," she said.

"Mom, I dropped out so I could help you," he said, finally, his voice soft, almost lower than the drone of the AC on the hot summer day.

"What?"

"Mom, your hospital bills aren't going to pay themselves. I can't work a full-time job, take care of you, and go to school. I tried, I did, but something had to give."

"Joe—" she started, and then she coughed, which turned

into a coughing fit, her body spasming in the passenger seat, and she hurriedly dug through her purse and found a tissue and put it over her mouth. The coughs died out, and she wiped her mouth, balling up the tissue and cramming it back into her purse.

"You shouldn't have," she said, finally, looking at him.

"It was an easy choice," he said. "I can always go back to school. But you need me. There's no one else. And without your job, your savings won't last forever. So I'm here."

"Joe, you can't sacrifice your future for me."

"I'm not sacrificing anything," he said. He glanced over at her. "You shouldered the burden for me. Now I'm doing it for you."

31

Joe got to the retirement home within an hour. The drive was a blur, of avoiding other cars, of zombies, of people. Betsy sat in the back seat of the Jeep. He had buckled her in as best he could, and Betsy didn't move. She was a good girl.

He did his best to not think of Anna. Of the fact that an hour ago she was fine, and now she was dead, or dying, and she would be back, as one of those things—

Joe focused on the road ahead of him. He had to get to his mom. He had to find her, and save her, and stay alive long enough for all the creatures to die off. Once they did, they could get out. Maybe someone would come in to rescue them. If the military had shut down the power, the cell service, the internet, it's because their plan worked. The info about Nile's plans had gotten out there and was spreading around. Journalists were doing their job.

That's what Joe focused on, as he piloted the Jeep around wrecks, and dead bodies, and the undead. He didn't focus on Wally. Or Anna. Or Helen. Or the thousands of other dead in the city—

It was your fault. You did this. That stuff was in a container until you let it out—

Joe didn't think about anything else, and he got to the retirement home safely. The parking lot was half-full, like normal, but it was quiet, down a long, mostly empty street. There was a mobile home park a little farther down, but there was no noise from it, at least not now.

He put Betsy back in her backpack, and she didn't struggle at all. He slid it on, and it was heavy, but he wanted her with him, and he didn't want her on the ground. That's where those things were, after he shot them, and they would kill her, and he wouldn't allow it. He'd die first.

The outside of the home seemed normal. Maybe they'd been unaffected. Maybe everyone inside had holed up, waiting for help. He'd be that help.

The power was out, and he had to force the automatic doors apart. No one was at the front desk, waiting for him. Otherwise, it was quiet. No smell, aside from the normal antiseptic stink, and no sounds. No muttering, no grunts of rage, no screaming as an undead creature tore apart his mother—

Stop, Joe. Stop it. Get to her, and it'll be alright.

And he was right, he had to get to her, but the thoughts still came, unbidden, thoughts of his mother being ripped apart on the ground, a group of dead monsters killing her, people she had known the day before. Someone from the group she played poker with, or her book club. They would grunt and mutter and stare at her with horrible rage and pull out her guts and leave her to die alone on the floor, and Joe would walk in, and find her there, nothing left, and it was *his fault*—

Joe pushed farther into the retirement home, listening as best he could for any signs of anything amiss. But there was nothing. He would find his mom. He would save her. They would get out of here. They would survive.

Then there was muttering from the hallway to his left and a zombie appeared, what was once an old man charged at him, his arms out to grab at Joe, to drag him down, to kill him, and Joe raised his rifle and took out the zombie's legs, and he fell to the ground with a thud. Joe took aim and shot its kneecaps, just to be sure, and the thing reached for him as he passed, but it was nothing, it stood in the way of his mom, it used to be human, but not anymore. He couldn't think that this man used to have a name, and a family, who paid for his stay here so that he'd be cared for.

No, he was an animal, to cripple, so that Joe could live.

Joe continued.

As he got deeper into the home, closer to his mother's room. The noises started. Mutters and murmurs, grunts and growls, and sounds of the undead. He smelt it now, too. The stench of death and decay, overwhelming the last time the place was cleaned, probably late last night. The thoughts of his mother rotting on her feet slid into his mind. She would join Anna, and Helen, and Wally, and everyone else he knew, they would all be dead, no, not dead, worse, undead. Wally would be there, reaching for Betsy for a reason he didn't know. Anna, with a bullet hole in her chin when she killed herself, so she wouldn't die slow, but now she couldn't die at all, Helen, who had worked hard and loved him, once upon a time. And Mom, who had gotten a drink from the tap this morning, she was a zombie too, and it was *his fault*—

No, no, stop it—

He pushed farther into the retirement home, his mind full of his mother, the dark, cold feelings in him pushed away, he couldn't give in, he would find her, he would save her.

She had protected him. She had raised him, after Dad died, after everything. She had worked herself to death for him, and he had failed her. Failed her in every way, only confirming that in her death.

You're a failure, Joe, you always have been, and now, you're just making sure you're consistent—

Joe cut off those thoughts, keeping his eyes up and ready for more creatures. A closed door to his right banged suddenly, and Betsy barked, surprised. Something muttered from behind the door, but Joe didn't answer it. He was almost to his mother's room, and he pictured her alive. He pictured her waiting in her room, alive and well, waiting for him. She would be scared, and he would usher her out of here. He would pay her back for all her sacrifices.

Crashing noises reached him from deeper in the home. Betsy barked, suddenly, and Joe turned, and shot the zombie coming at him from behind. Quiet this one was, and it fell, and he shot it in the legs just to be sure. His gun clicked empty, and he dropped the cartridge, and pulled another from the ammo bag, and jammed it in the rifle until it clicked.

He scanned all around him, but he was alone again.

His mom's room was close, just up the hallway and to the left, and he forced himself to stay slow, to stay careful. He wouldn't fail now. He'd help her. He'd save her.

Her door was there. He crept up to it, and tested the handle. It was locked. She was inside, she had to be.

"Mom?" he asked, to the door. He waited, holding his breath, listening.

No answer.

"Mom?"

Still nothing.

He tried the door again, but it was locked—

I'm coming, Mom, I'll save you—

He smashed the handle with the butt of his gun, once, twice, and then it shattered, and the lock broke, and the door swung open. Joe looked backward to see if there were any more zombies coming from behind, but he was alone for now. He stepped inside.

"Mom?" he asked, but there was nothing. No sounds at all.

And then he saw her. She waited in the corner. She was waiting for him.

*

The travel back to Helen's apartment had been rough. The streets were getting worse by the hour, as more and more zombies roamed, and more derelict vehicles clogged the roads. Soon he'd have to resort to going by foot or bicycle.

He'd stopped at the local grocery store, Lloyd's, the one he'd worked at for a spell as a teenager. He'd grabbed all the bottled water he could find, plus all the water purifier filters and containers. The place hadn't been empty, but he had kneecapped the few zombies inside, and loaded up everything he could fit into the Jeep, along with Betsy and his mom.

His mom hadn't been very helpful, but it wasn't her fault. She'd done her best. She always had, from the moment Joe was born.

The food and water would carry them for a while. Give him the time to sort their way out of this.

"Like anoth—anoth— gla—merlot?" muttered his mom from the couch. She struggled against the ropes from time to time. He'd had to tie her up, to protect himself. And her.

He'd barred the door to the bathroom, just to be on the safe side. Helen was still in there.

Joe would figure something out, he would.

They only had each other.

32

"—Nile's valuation has now gone over three trillion dollars, having surpassed Apple, as the most valuable company on Earth, in the wake of the US ruling officially allowing the dead to work, even in the wake of the report of Nile's involvement—"

The TV switched off. Olivia turned to see Ron holding the remote.

"Don't know why you're watching that," said Ron.

"It's important to keep up with things," said Olivia. "I want to know what's going on."

"What did I say? I told you what would happen, Liv."

"Yes, yes, I know. The great oracle predicted it—but your vague guesses are not the same as the news, honey."

Ron sighed. "It's all the same, in the end. The big companies do what they want. It was only a matter of time before the government rolled over."

Olivia looked at him for a second, and then away, at the blank screen of the television.

"I don't think we should order from Nile anymore," she said, finally.

"What? Why?"

Olivia stared at him. "Why? What were we just talking about? They're using those things as slaves. Firing half their workforce. I know we're only one house, but we should put our money where our mouth is. I don't feel right giving them our business."

Ron stared at her for a second. "Honey—"

"What?" she asked.

"I mean, do you think any of the other companies won't be doing this soon enough?"

"But they're not now—"

"But what if they are?" asked Ron. "What are we going to do, then?"

"I don't think everyone will use them," said Olivia.

"Are you kidding me? Of course they will. As soon as they figure out how, they'll do the same thing. Anything to cut costs. I don't see a difference in buying our toilet paper from Nile, or from Target, or from Walmart. It's all the same."

"It's not the same—"

"Well, we already have a delivery on the way from Nile. Should be here any second."

"What?"

"We needed paper towels, so I ordered them," said Ron. "I'll order them from somewhere else next time, if it bothers you that much."

"One of the—you know—is going to deliver it!"

"Well, yes," said Ron. "It'll be fine. Better get used to it."

Olivia's phone buzzed in her pocket, and she pulled it out to see the notification on her doorbell camera.

"It's here!" she whispered.

"You don't have to be quiet, Liv," said Ron. Olivia opened up the app to see a dead woman standing on her doorstep, holding a box. The woman's skin was pale, and red lines extended out from her eyes and mouth. She wore a jumpsuit that covered the rest of her body, with a thin metal collar around her neck.

"She's just standing there," said Olivia.

"It," said Ron. "It's just standing there."

The creature then lowered the box to the floor of their front porch, and then slowly turned and walked away, disappearing out of the view of the camera. Olivia scrambled to her feet and hurried to the front window, just in time to see the dead woman stumble back into a van, the door closing shut behind her.

"She can't be driving," said Olivia.

"Automated vehicle," said Ron. "Drives itself."

"How does it know—"

"Does it matter?" asked Ron. He went to the front door.

"What are you doing?" asked Olivia, her voice still quiet.

"I'm getting our paper towels," said Ron.

"Wait, honey—"

But Ron had already opened the front door and grabbed the box from the porch. It was a big box, but light, and he pulled it inside.

"Should you be touching it?" asked Olivia.

"Being dead isn't contagious, dear," said Ron, ripping the box open and pulling out the package of six paper towel rolls. He broke down the box just as quick and threw it on the stack near the garage. "Easy as pie."

Olivia stared as Ron took the paper towels into the kitchen. She looked out the window. The van was already gone.

No different from their normal Nile deliveries. Someone shows up, quickly drops off a package, and then disappears. It's not like she knew the delivery people anyway, or ever spoke to them. She never tipped them, or left them snacks.

Maybe Ron was right. What was the difference?

Maybe—maybe it was better.

No human was mistreated this way. Olivia had heard the horror stories of people having to pee on the road. Of not driving safely. And the people in the warehouses, working through hell to pack all the boxes.

That dead woman—I mean, yeah, it was ghastly, seeing them at first. But the dead woman felt nothing.

She needed nothing.

Maybe it was better.

It didn't hurt anyone.

ENJOY DEAD END?

Sign up here to be notified about Robbie's next novel!

robbiedorman.com/newsletter

And don't forget to leave a review. Reviews are a direct way to help your favorite creators. We appreciate it.

ACKNOWLEDGEMENTS

Thank you to my wife Kim, for her patience and support, and my team of beta readers: Andrew, Carrie, Matt, Megan, and Yousef. Thank you for reading.

ABOUT THE AUTHOR

Robbie Dorman believes in horror. Dead End is his fourteenth novel. When not writing, he's podcasting, playing video games, or walking his dog. He lives in Florida with his wife, Kim.

You can follow Robbie on all social media @robbiedorman

His website is robbiedorman.com

Subscribe to his newsletter at robbiedorman.com/newsletter